THE DEMO TAPES

The Demo Tapes
Anthology 2017-2020

DANIEL TRIUMPH

Chochma Arts Ltd.

Publishing Information

(Author's Original Publishing Page)

Copyright © 2020 by Daniel Triumph

All rights reserved. No part of this book may be reproduced in any manner whatsoever without written permission except in the case of brief quotations embodied in critical articles and reviews.

First Printing, 2020
Published in Canada
September 9/10, 2020
First Edition (Revision 1)

For further information, please address

Daniel Triumph
@danielltriumph
www.danieltriumph.com

ChochmaArts@outlook.com
@ChochmaArts
www.chochmaarts.ca

Cover and Interior design by Daniel Triumph

If you find any spelling, textual or other errors, please email ChochmaArts@outlook.com *so that they may be addressed and remedied in the next edition!*

Thank you to
My mother, my grandmother,
Nick, and all sorts of other friends and family.

Additional Thanks

Additional thanks to everyone who helped edit the Portfolios that would help me enter my university honours program, and come to comprise this anthology over the past three years, as well as those who workshopped some of these pieces within the program itself. There are also those with whom I ran tabletop role playing games, where many of these early ideas and concepts were stress-tested in a live play environment.

Contents

Dedication — vi
Additional Thanks — vii

The Hero and the Star — 1

Alice and Finch – Chapter 1: Primary Dawn — 2

The Solune Prince - Chapter 4: Mental/Physical Resistance — 6

The Solune Prince - Chapter 5: [Excerpt] — 10

The Djeb Guard — 11

Wavering — 15

Of Commonplaces: An Essai for Montaigne — 20

The Solune Prince - Chapter 10: The Aftermath of Thought; (or The N'Tariel Talent) — 23

Digression IIII - The Legendary Event: A Brief Account from Chloe Rhye — 28

Span — 31

Inck — 38

Kēmeía — 42

The Solune Prince – Chapter [unknown]: Projection Exercise — 47

Raze	49
Mariça	54
The Young Spectator	72
One Man's Fantasy – Sermon I	76
Starman	78
Alice and Finch – Chapter 13: Sluggish Mind	86
Alice and Finch: Archetypal Recapitulation	93
The Youth of Yaska May Däwngale	99
WHAT WAS IT LIKE? THE FUTURE.	101
grunge	105
A Canto of Alexandre Dirge	106
PS Y CHOSIS	110
Shade the Past	111
"There Was a Soul"	112
Wraith Hail	113
The Solune Prince - Chapter 6: The Assassin; or The Lussa Part 1	116
The Capital	120
Pressing	122
The Long Haiku	124

	Lussa Confederation [Excerpts]	125
	Dawngale and Zeth	127
	String Quartet	130
	The Solune Prince – Chapter 41-42: Regimen I-II	134

Back 141
About The Author 142

The Hero and the Star

Thousands of years ago, a star fell from the sky. It was unlike a dead shooting star. It was alive. It landed on the planet, and the ancient people encountered it, and came to fear it.

Luckily, the first person to find it was a town hero, a man of virtue. The star landed in the square, and it took on the hero's image as its own. For the citizens, the transformation and the copy, it was all very uncanny. They accused the star of being a demon, and captured it.

The hero feared for the star. He knew that it would be charged will any form of frivolity, and that the ancient nation would decide they should kill it. Standing around the star's prison, and surrounded by his people, the hero took a risk to save the life of the star.

The hero gave a great laugh, and then pointed to the cage. "You fools, you have captured the wrong person, for I am the star, and he is the true hero!

The star was cunning. It said, "Indeed, I am your noble hero, please free me!"

The hero gave the star a smile, and then ran away. Half of the people pursued, and the other half hastened to free the one they thought to be their hero. The star needed to find help, so it said in a heroic voice, "I will chase down the imposter! Leave it to me!" And gave chase. The two heroes ran about the city, each claiming to be chasing the other.

The true hero stopped at his house to rest. He hid and watched through his doorway. The city calmed. The star, seeing that the hero was missing, assured everyone that he had chased the imposter out of the city. Then he patrolled in search of the hero, fearful at the civilization before him, fearful that his impostering would be uncovered.

Finally, the star noticed the hero in his doorway. He beckoned. The star approached, and the hero pulled him in. Safe inside the house, the hero told the star to journey out of the city and return to his home. The star told him, "I need energy," so the hero gave food and drink, the star thanked the hero, but took only water. Then the star left the city under the guise of the hero, and returned unto the skies. The hero watched as he ascended to the night sky. It became the southern star, the beacon that the ancient hero later used to guide us to our current land.

Alice and Finch – Chapter 1: Primary Dawn

Ever since she appeared in the capital, Alice was always a point of interest. During her childhood, she had passively garnered followers, children in the neighbourhood and later others from around the entire city. Alice was an energetic girl. She wasn't entirely coherent, but she was very driven and children seemed to find value in that. Adults would watch her warily and some would even keep their children away from her. It was the unusual appearance. Alice had an obvious and striking look to her. Her hair was brightly coloured, less Solune-brown and more sandy-orange. Usually, her eyes were a deep maroon, but when she got excited or angry they would become an astonishing red. But, the real reason why adults avoided her was because of her unpredictability, paired with her tooth and nail.

Alice was of the mysterious desert people from the east, a Plainkind. She had extra canines, longer and thicker than any Solune's. They often hid behind her stretch-marked cheeks, but when she smiled they never failed to come out. Her nails were not only long, but claw-like. And her free spirit made many worry; what would she do next? Even worse, there were the rumours, whispers passed behind scornful faces. Had she ever used those claws? Hurt someone? Maybe killed someone? And with a spirit such as hers, whatever she may or may not have done obviously didn't affect her morality. Did she even have respect for us common folk?

But those were only rumours, right?

Finch had heard all of these things, and so he'd avoided the southern area of the city. His father, Ilias, had told Finch that she was a dangerous monster. Sometimes his friend Artus would invite him along to go visit her, but he always refused. He liked to listen to what his father said.

Finch was walking home from the library with an armful of books. His father had been homeschooling him; the primary method of education in Murdock city. He'd sent the boy with a list, and Finch had also taken some books he was personally interested in. Unlike most children, he wasn't interested in the Prince's adventure series or Gwen-hime's Tales of Conquest. Finch sought only Natural Studies textbooks. He also liked finding books from outside of the city, from academics such Joss Resz, Bradley Jeremy, and Azure Shion.

He was halfway to his house now, and the books were starting to strain his arms. He might have taken too many personal picks.

"Aww man..."

Finch knew he'd have to rest at some point before reaching his house. He saw a bench and decided that now was as good a time as any. He sat down and put the pile of books beside him. It almost reached up to his shoulders. Finch closed his eyes and caught his breath. He had definitely taken too many.

"Hello there!" A voice said.

Finch jolted, immediately tensing up. He turned to his left side, and saw the top of a head hiding behind the pile of books. He didn't remember seeing anyone there while sitting down, but the person looked so small that he wasn't sure if he'd missed them altogether.

"Umm," Like most children, Finch had little sense for pleasantries and got right to the point, "How did you get there?"

"Oh, I saw you sit down, so I came and sat next to you. Or at least I tried. I didn't want to sit on your books!" The voice replied.

"Oh."

He could still only see the small person's hair. It was an unusual colour. He and his father had black hair, but most of the other people in the city had blonde or light brown hair. This person had blazingly bright orange-yellow hair.

"Your hair looks like a fire." He said.

"I know. Isn't it cool?" The small person replied, sounding excited.

"Yeah. Hey, can you stop hiding behind the books?" Finch asked.

"No, you're scary."

Finch stopped, confused. No one had ever called him scary. Maybe it was because he was already twelve. He was only three years from being an adult! Maybe that was why. But he wasn't sure, so he asked.

"How am I scary?"

"Your hair is so dark. And your eyes too!" The small person said.

He had never thought about this. He looked just like his dad, but thinking back now it seemed no one else looked like them. Finch became very confused, but he was still more curious than anything.

"If you don't show me your face," He started, thinking, "I'll just stand up so I can see it!"

"Oh..." The person said, "Okay fine."

The small person leaned back slowly, peeking from behind the books.

"You're a girl!" Finch said. It was hard to tell by voice with the younger kids, he found.

The small girl nodded. Finch decided that *she* was the unusual one of the two. She had darker skin, like she'd been in the sun for... forever! And the bright hair made her eyebrows and eyelashes stand out.

"Hi! Well, what's your name? How old are you?" She asked the two most common questions a child could ask.

Finch was used to answering them, "My name is Finch Dirge Zeth, I'm twelve."

"That's a strange name. Out of all the kids I've talked to, you have the most weirdest name."

"So?" He said, "What's yours then?"

"I'm called Alice! Alice May Dawngale. I'm fourteen." She said proudly. "That's the name my mom told me a long time ago."

"What do you mean a long time ago?" He was curious now.

"Well, my mom has passed away." She said almost robotically.

Finch had a feeling she had said this sentence many times, to many people. But he was more interested in what was said than how it was said.

"Wow. Mine too," Finch replied looking forward, "It's just me and my dad."

"Hey, that's cool though!" She said, excited. He noticed that she always seemed a little excited.

"What do you mean cool? Almost everyone has a dad."

"No..."

Finch couldn't believe what she was saying.

"You have no parents?!" He yelled, surprised.

Alice pulled her head down into her chest, "No... It's just me."

Finch felt bad. He started to think what it would be like without his dad. How would he get food? How would he learn? Just read? Who would he talk to? Who would take care of him? It would be all him, he'd have to do all of those things. Finch thought about Alice doing that all alone, with no mom or dad. He thought about her going into the forest all alone, hunting mobile moose or finding emango trees and climbing them for the fruit, without anyone to catch her. He wondered where she lived, did she sleep outside in the rain?

"Hey, are you okay? Are you crying?" Alice asked.

"No." He replied, wiping his face.

"Well, it was nice meeting you, but I have to go." She said.

"Okay, goodbye." He replied.

"It's not goodbye. It's, see you later! So, I'll see you later!" She said and then jumped up.

The girl was really small. Finch didn't believe that she was two years older than him. He stood up too, watching Alice as she left, heading south. South.

"Oh no! My dad!"

Finch had remembered the monster from the south. That was it! She was the monster! Alice Dawngale was the monster that he was supposed to keep away from! He grabbed his books and ran home, worried.

Every child lies to their parents, even more so if they know they'll get in trouble if they tell the truth. Finch slowed to a walk as he neared his home. He could see it at the end of the cobblestone road, right on the corner. He wasn't sure if he should tell his dad. He didn't know if he'd get in trouble, what he would do. Finch knew that his dad always knew best though.

"Right. So if dad always knows best, then I can tell him and he will do what is the right thing to do." He said, stumbling over his sentence nervously.

He got to the door, pulled the latch with his elbow and nudged it open.

The Solune Prince - Chapter 4: Mental/Physical Resistance

"Why did I say anything? Was it nerves perhaps?"

Chloe exited the castle. The city had been built around the stone building's backside, which meant that in order to get into the city, she had to exit from the front, walk half a kilocubit, and re-enter through the impenetrable main gate. In concept, it was an effective way to keep the citizens safe from bandits and raids, but in everyday life, it was nothing more than a detour.

To assemble a research team, the university would have been a good first stop. It was not where Chloe went. Her default response to meeting new people was simple—don't. She was aware that such an approach was flawed and impossible given her task, but that didn't mean she couldn't procrastinate. Chloe, instead, headed for the home of someone she did know.

The door opened after a few tolls on the bell. A pale man with dark hair and bright eyes opened the door. He was an entire head shorter than Chloe, so eye contact was a chore for both of them.

"Good morning, Chloe."

"Did you just wake?"

"Yes, but not because of you. I live with the earliest bird in the tree. As a result, I enjoy waking up an hour before even the sun on a daily basis. Even off days."

"Right. Where is she?"

Finch, Chloe remembered, had married somewhere between three and seven years ago. (Her memory for such things was limited.)

He said, "Well, while it is a weekend, she should be leaving..." he looked to the sun, "A little while ago. Alice!"

Finch called out behind him, and a muscled, bare-chested woman skipped to the door, her upper half jamming itself into a top that seemed too small.

When she had dressed, she said, "Hi Chloe, I have to go! Visit me some time?" And then sprinted away.

They watched for a few moments as she ran towards the heart of the city, and then Chloe said, "Ah, can we sit maybe?"

"Sure, I happen to own a kitchen table."

They sat and caught up. Finch had left the guard to study kemia and physics. Chloe told him about her trip, and the Lussa, and then finally her current mission.

"Oh nice. Isn't that the whole thing you've been complaining about this past month?"

"Yes. I'm wondering if you know of anyone I could bring. Anyone academic."

"You should check out the university."

"Yes, but who for?"

Finch considered. He really didn't know anyone. "Oh, well, you could always try my cousin Alexandre."

"Yeah? What field?"

"Kemia, but more recently the hormonal differences between the kingdom's various ethnicities. We are all quite unique, it seems. Especially the N'Tarial, and Riley like myself."

"Oh. Is he married? Okay with leaving town for a few months?"

"She should be fine."

"Hmm."

They ended up having tea, and then eventually lunch before Chloe finally stood to leave. Before she went out the door, Finch added, "She's just out of prison a couple of years ago though, so she can be a little rough around the edges."

"Ah..." Chloe lost what little momentum she had at this. *I guess it would be right to assume that she is going to be something of a hassle.*

As usual, the university's flora was entirely overgrown. The grass was knee-high, and vines draped over trees and buildings. There had been a set of large stone letters that read 'THE SOLUNE ACADEMY' but the rock was now entirely covered in lichen and leafed plants. *At least it is still readable. I can understand everything else, but why not clean off the lettering?*

The paths that led from building to building were where the health and safety concerns really began. The cobble had a thick layer of moss, and it would detach and slide if you stepped on it incorrectly. The liberal and academic solution was simply to put up a sign, 'slipping hazard.' Luckily for the faculty and the students, there was someone more conservative and practical who had added 'shovel walkways' to the list of janitorial tasks.

The only thing that kept the path up to municipal code was the footpath of stone that ran through the moss, wide enough only for one person, and cleared weekly.

Chloe sighed. *I love it here.*

She headed first to the administration building. Then, because it was locked and unlit, she went to the biokem building to see if anyone was there. Also locked. *The lounge building maybe?*

There was only two people in the lounge. *What is going on?* Chloe surveyed the building. Lunch tables, some longer seats, a café area, and a woman who looked like she was from the Djeb. Chloe looked around and saw a calendar.

Oh no, it's Secast, ah, it is the weekend. Of course everything is closed!

"Hey!"

Chloe spun around so fast that she lost her balance and fell forward. She was caught by the Djeb woman.

"Oh, ah, thank you."

"Sure! Are you a student here?"

Chloe looked at her. She had sand coloured hair, and down-turned eyes. Her skin seemed a touch darker and thicker than her own. Not that much different than other Djeb people she had seen—not even that much different than Solune when she thought about it. The woman also had the universal Djeb neutral expression, one of both constant joy and concern.

"I'm Alumni."

"Oh! Even better! Would you like to do an interview with me?

Chloe squinted, "Not right now. I am, ah, I'm looking for Alexandre Dirge, but I do not think she's here today."

"Oh, probably not."

"You, you're a little frustrating to engage."

"Why's that?" The Djeb smiled.

Chloe frowned, "Do you need something?"

"Yes—but wait, aren't you busy?"

"Not if Alex isn't here. Not until next day."

"Wonderful! My name is Senica, I'm an anthropologist from the south!"

"You mean the west, where the Djeb is."

"Nope," Senica grinned, "south."

That does not make sense, there's only a mountain to the south. Chloe decided, despite the contradiction, not to get into it.

"I came here to do some research and ask people some questions."

"I am not in a good mood, Senica."

"Oh, well... okay."

They parted ways. Chloe went homeward.

On the way back, passing through the market, she saw someone with short black hair and pale skin. *Finch? No, far too tall... and feminine. Who...*

The woman was arguing with a stall keeper. Chloe got close enough to hear.

"Look, I've even used these before. I've worked with the guard too."

Chloe saw that she was at a smith, a swords booth.

"It doesn't matter, you need a permit." Then he added under his breath, "This is why I hate coming to market."

Chloe, feeling bored, failed and frustrated, decided to step in and see if could help one of them; she just wasn't sure which one. *I just need... an outlet, a distraction. Maybe I can solve this, or at least try.*

"What is, ah, what's happening here?" She slipped up in her first sentence, and the Riley noticed. She also noticed Chloe's nervous tone of voice.

"This Riley wants to get a hard edge sword, but lacks the permit. She's not allowed to purchase a weapon, no one can without a permit!"

Chloe thought for a moment, and then said, "No one?"

His eyes widened with recognition, but he quickly returned to his unhappy expression. "Well, there are exceptions."

"Not exceptions. They are clear and in the law. There are no exceptions in Solune governing. And," she turned to the Riley. Her speech was beginning to speed up, she was reaching her limit. "What of you? Who are you?"

The Riley spat on the dirt. "I am Jutt. Soon, you would call me Dr. Dirge."

"Are you Alexandre Dirge?"

"Don't worry about it, Prince." Alexandre turned to leave.

Wait! No, I need to say something more forceful than wait. "No."

Alexandre glanced back apathetically and stepped away. Chloe, who was both taller and broader, grabbed the Riley's wrist.

"I have been looking for you. You are a student of Kemia, right?"

Alexandre tried unsuccessfully to wrench away.

Chloe sort of lost herself in thought. I am stronger than someone who wishes to wield a sword. I wonder why? Perhaps that is why she wants one, because she's weak? Wait... Chloe remembered what Finch had told her. Why was she imprisoned?

"I'm not working for the castle."

She wrenched again.

"No, not the castle, I am going on an expedition to study the Lussa, I, ah, I'm assembling a research team."

"So?"

Chloe let go. Alexandre skulked away, rubbing her wrist only when she thought she was out of sight. Chloe still saw. She turned back to the blacksmith and said goodbye, and scanned the market.

" ... "

Chloe stood in the middle of the bustling market and entered a state of deep thought.

The Solune Prince - Chapter 5: [Excerpt]

...

...

Why did I let her go?

Because I did not have an answer for her.

What do I do now?

Find a reason, and give it to her. Figure out what will entice her to join.

Certainly she has not given the offer a fair chance.

Certainly!

When Chloe finally came back to reality, she was extremely disoriented. She opened her eyes and looked around, getting a feel for her situation. It was still afternoon. She was still in the market. The sounds returned to her, the bustle of trade. She had unconsciously moved to a bench. There was a child on the bench with her, and he was poking her face. She was so tall, however, that the child had to stand on the bench to reach.

Chloe didn't like this, so she told him to stop. He sort of yelped and then ran away. As usual, she recounted that which was useful from her bout of deep thought.

Alexandre did not say "no!" she said, and rather arbitrarily, that she was not going to work for the castle. I said that it was an expedition, and all she had said was, "So?"

She held onto the fragment of hope.

The Djeb Guard

We are they, we watch the city.

We are the ones who respond.
If they come with hands open to take, or hands closed to hit.
If they come with words that are false, or words that are threats.
We are the ones who respond.

We are here, we watch the city.
We walk overnight, we walk overday.
We walk along paths, we walk overland.
If you need any help, call the guard of the Djeb.

—

They call to us, of a winged creature. I respond.
They come to me, they fear the unknown.
I stand for them, I am their safety.
I must remain calm.

The guards' process.
Step one is discover. What is the conflict?
Step two is confirm. What is the nature?
Step three is intervene. Can it be done by reason?

Step one is discover. I speak to them, what is the conflict?
The creature entered the city, It isn't too big.
The creature entered the city, it looks just like us.
She is smaller though.

I speak to them. What has it done?
Voices, murmurs, shrugs, suspicion.

Wings, a sword, teeth, suspicion.
I cannot act on suspicion.

Step two is confirm. I must speak to the creature.
She says she is Yaska, from the east.
She says she is passing through, to an inn.
She says— I interrupt her.

Yaska May Dawngale,
Yaska, one of the Solune Legends.
Yaska, a hero of the East.
Yaska, unbelievable might.
Yaska, of the Plainkind.

Step three is intervene. I must reason with the people.
The Plainkind has not caused any trouble.
The Plainkind should not be suspicious.
The Plainkind is a Solune hero.

—

The flames rise into the sky, and we respond.
How could this happen, here on the shore?

"Get the people out of the district."
The flames cannot be stopped.
They spread along buildings and homes.
I watch.
What can we do?
"Hannah, focus on the people."

I focus on the people.
I focus on the process.
The guard's process.

Step one is discover.
The conflict is not the fire, it's the people escaping it.
Step two is confirm.
The nature is not to rescue the homes, it's to rescue the people.

Step three is intervene. Can it be done by reason?

I say, "take them to the eastern district."
I say, "take them across the canal."
I say, "take them, lead them there."

Guards discover people in homes, so they don't get trapped.
Guards create checkpoints, to confirm their path, and their safety.
Guards intervene with inns, to find places for them.

The people are safe, but the fires still burn.
It moves towards the east.
It moves towards the canal.

—

It's too big for a line of buckets.
But we try nonetheless.

I take an empty bucket,
I fill it with seawater,
I pass it down the line,
I take an empty bucket...

The rhythm of buckets,
has become automatic.

And I stare out into the sea.
The islands of mountains.
The dim of the sky.
The winged shadow.
Rising from the east.

It shot from the city, into the air.
It shot from the air, over the sea.
It shot from the sea, onto an island.

Suddenly, the tip of the mountaintop breaks off.
A feat of strength, it's lifted from its perch.
I watch as it's launched into the air.
I watch as it falls into the sea, just off the shore.
I watch the waves, they echo off the island.
They head towards our shoreline.

I point, I shout, "tidal wave"

The guards follow the path of the people.
We exit to the eastern district.
And the waves come to the flames.

Water hits the shore and rises,
Momentum cracks against the beaches.
The waves hit the buildings,
And the flames drown.

—

"Do you think my wave did more damage than the fire might have?
Hannah shrugged, "a drenched and damaged structure is better than a pile of ash."

Wavering

Wavering

A numb pain flowed from her arm. It made her uncomfortable. She looked where the branch jut out from betwixt the two bones in her forearm.
    She was in a pit, a lush bright brown hole of moss and grass and dirt;
dirt from where the roots of a tree had torn the top layers of soil from the earth.
It was long covered over now,
Long enough that there was now moss and patches of grass and small plants
and long enough that there was this fucking adolescent tree.
This tree whose branch had intruded in on her arm.
She failed to take hold of her senses, Her mind'd left her in an uncanny state.

In the distance, it seemed, a hazy figure, blue like the sky, moved with purpose;
Then it stopped.

Ah, the King is awake.

The voice touched her ears, but seemed to skip the formality of exercising her nervous system.
    a strange feeling
This person was not her sister.
She didn't much like the voice thath'd interjected itself into her mind.

The person looked around, a blue glowing blur,
twelve percent of your blood is shared with Mother Earth.

It was definitely a man, but his voice wasn't particularly deep.
    It's pitch was higher even than Natasha's, although, her tone was low due to the immense height of her trachea. She is very tall.
    Janna blinked, slowly. Her eyelids were sore. She tried to focus. nothing worked.

You have fluid in your eyes, focusing will not help you.

Janna became irritated with the glowing man in front of her.

You'll be fine in this line, he said. In certain distant timelines, you lose more...you lose too much. A drop of cobalt fell from his face.

He stood over her, outlined in azure. Through her wavering eyes, she could see wisps, branching lines of light coming from him.

She didn't like any of it
so she told him, You can leave now.

He said, I came to ask for your help.

You thought now would be the best time?
Take advantage of me because I'm dying?
You can take that straight to the abyss.

Umm, no... I mean, as far as I can tell, you aren't going to die. and even if you were, I don't know if I could really help you.

Janna tried to focus on the figure, but her vision waved.
She was pissed off. What an annoying man, like a man to be this indecisive. He isn't talking so fancy anymore. God damn, a fucking actor.
She said, I don't know what you want, so either spit it out so that I can disagree with it, or leave me alone.

I am the Servant of Tendrils, I can see into future timelines... although too far ahead there are too many tendrils to know anything.
From what I can tell we can benefit the next few years if we work together.
You have influence, and an open mind.

Janna sneered, Not that open.

She looked at her arm. It'd become crimson. Where the hell is Chloe?

Why don't you help me first.
I'll talk to your dumbass after
when I'm not attached to goddamn plant.

Tendrils frowned, I thought that you would agree, but... maybe my reading was wrong.

At this Janna cursed the sky.
The idiot is talking fancy shit again.
Then she cursed the being in front of her.
For being a fraud.

Yeah, maybe you are wrong.
So why don't you help me—by leaving me alone.
Tendrils' teeth glowed, irritated.
I didn't come here to help you! I need your help! Don't you understand what I am?

Janna's head slumped to face him.
A fucking glowstick?
I can tell exactly what you are! She judged, I can tell you're an actor, a fraud, you're presenting me with a false version of yourself,
A false reality!
I don't want it!
Leave me alone, you said I'll survive? Well that's fucking great. That's all I want from you. Fuck off!

No! He shouted, flaring to the colour of lightning.
No. he calmed.
no.
I'm a Servant of the conscious world,
I see the future...in a sense. But I can't affect anything in the way people like you can.
I can communicate, I can,
with people whose minds aren't as firmly attached to the physical world, even if it is only while they are in states like this,
I can communicate with those like you.

Then she opened her eyes again.
She said,
and then she didn't.
She said,
Well, I'd be far more willing to work with you if you were more honest like that all the time.
And shed a tear;pearl (of wisdom)

You will help me then?
Janna closed her eyes, and then her world focused.

"She has gone catatonic. Oh good, the bleeding has slowed! Although, it is probably from being catatonic."

Janna opened her eyes. Her younger sister was kneeling over her. Behind, her older sister loomed. Janna saw that she was also bleeding in the forearm.

"Oh, look Natasha, she's awake! Actually, ah, maybe that's not so good. Hey, you can take a little pain, I guess?"

Janna felt a pinch as Chloe's arms moved over her wound. She said nothing.

"Actually, it's better to be awake when you're hurt like this. I think. Hey Natasha, do you have a, ah, do you have a knife? Of course you do, we just used it, haah... Can you hold the top, I don't want it to move until I'm done."

Janna closed her eyes, but the Servant of Tendrils didn't return. She wondered if he knew her answer?

"She is dead now," Natasha said.

"Hey, wake up!"

Janna gave a shallow nod.

"I wish you would open your eyes. Look Natasha, just hold that and I'll cut it, and then I can pull it—Ah!"

It was dark for a long time, and then she saw blue.

"Oh no."

"Do you think she will be all right?"

"I think so. I'm not really, ah, I don't actually... I'm not a doctor so..."

She heard another voice, "Can we move her yet?"

"You know," Janna blinked back into focus, "for a Servant, Tendrils sure is a dumbass."

Chloe gave her a perplexed look, "Not Death?"

Janna laughed weakly,
I think I prefer Tendrils to Death

Of Commonplaces: An Essai for Montaigne

As the ancients* say, "Possessed with hellish torment, / I master magics five"

Are there Commonplaces in my generation? That universal, perhaps conversational, well of references and information. Is it gone? Have we lost our *topoi*? Is *topoi* the right word? Perhaps not. I will for purposes of this essai, appropriate Aristotle's term.

Let topoi be defined as a topic which one can invoke in conversation with nearly anyone, and on which all have opinions, usually preconceived. Weather is, perhaps, the most universal topoi, under this definition. Family and occupation follow. Sports may also be a topos, depending. It seems that a topos that is deviant from the mainstream and particular to young people becomes the defining feature of what is called a "sub-culture." Usually, a sub-culture orients themselves around music, like punk or rock and roll. Punk is dead, but "metal is forever" (Halford, 1988). Each culture has its own set of topoi. Etiquette, manners, may have been one. Television, I have been told, used to have only a few dominant channels, so everyone was familiar with a set of shows. Certain religions had common stories, and met at common times to explore and share their given mythos. Many cultures *had* folklore; gnomes and elves hiding beneath toadstools. The Commonplaces of my generation seem to have disintegrated. Perhaps postmodernism truly did permeate the culture (rather than being simply a rhetorical deviant of modernism) and grand narratives are all gone. We are left with fragmented and unrelatable childhoods, which have become technology-assisted isolation.

Sociologists and scholars like Benet Davetian speak of "Low Context," and "High Context" cultures. In high context cultures, there is a lot of assumed etiquette, behaviour, and knowledge. They can be inaccessible to outsiders. France. Japan. Poland too, I hear. Low context cultures are the opposite; they are very direct. Little information is assumed. They are easier to visit and immigrate to. America is a prime example; here in Canada things are similar. A lack of Commonplaces. Education, which should be gold for topoi cultivation (after all, what are the classics of literature but topoi?) has come to fail at this task—precisely at a time when young people need community more than ever. Loneliness and depression statistics surge. Suicide too, according to Dr. Twenge and Dr. Haidt. High school taught Shakespeare. My peers and

I dozed through it, and thus fail to remember the bard. And so, lacking topoi, I cannot—as past figures like Michel de Montaigne, Sir Cornwallis the Younger, or Francis Bacon did—reference what is during my time Commonplace. Aristotelian assumptions, Cartesian meditations, Platonic beratements, Seneca's assertions, Solomon's Proverbs, Cicero's arguments, Homer's longwinded passages; I cannot expect to get away with mentioning such figures—especially uncited—without frustrating a reader (—though apparently I can get away with early print style page-long sentences, as good Cornwallis did). So where might a person find Commonplaces? What words of wisdom have I absorbed, *memoria*? Perhaps music is the topoi of our age; as the music industry auto-tunes art, lyrics become a universal. Where once we had bards and Beowulf, now we have Kanye and Star Wars. Do I wear my sunglasses at night? I digress. And me? What Commonplace wisdom literature can I proclaim?

"Possessed with hellish torment,
I master magics five."

"Five Magics" from the platinum-certified *Rust in Peace*. Is this a topoi? Perhaps in one "sub-culture." But worse, there is the inside-joke. What are the "Magics Five?" "Alchemy, wizardry, sorcery, thermatology, and electricity." Included is a branch of therapeutic medicine, and a field of physics respectively. Magic? And like Dave Mustaine,* I extend this idea far beyond its original intent. This is the "inside-joke" where only those *familiar with the inside of my head* will understand what I mean. This is the opposite of topoi.

The explanation. English Literature is something of a branch of the Humanities. Wide education. The original Liberal Arts complimented the two "Queen" disciplines: philosophy and theology. The Trivium were the "humanities:" grammar, logic, and rhetoric. The Quadrivium were the "sciences:" arithmetic, geometry, astronomy, and...music. The Trivium and Quadrivium made up the Liberal arts. By the simple arithmetic (counting), I conflate the subjects thusly: The two Queens, the Trivium, the Quadrivium, the Magics Five. This is what a logician would call a valid yet unsound argument. Magics Five, like Liberal Arts, is a broad term. Perhaps it is poetry? Or perhaps thermatology, or romanticism, or transcendentalism, or whatever original theologies William Blake or Isaac Newton held to. Thus, I call upon the following topoi:

"Possessed with hellish torment,
I master magics five."

Mastery is key. Without my excessive explanation, how could I assume a person knows these particular Megadeth lyrics off-hand; and how can I then go further use those lines as a launching point for inspiration? Certainly, I cannot use it as a proof for a statement in an essai. Unlike the essaist Montaigne, I have not memorized sections of Plutarch and Homer. I have memorized bits of Mustaine and Halford. I know *of* what the old Renaissance Humanists referenced, but I'm hardly as widely read as them. They, the educated classes, had classical topoi of learning. They even had a Commonplace language: Latin. This is the brilliance of the commonplace book as put forward by Erasmus. A less learnèd individual could keep up with the others in their writing and oratory through the reference of their very own hand-picked collection of topoi.

Have we anything near such Commonplaces? I could tell you all about Plato, or H.D., maybe Milton or Faulkner. What a strange time to be educated. *Certes* then, the Commonplaces of our age are Trump, Marvel, and Game of Thrones. People know these things, or know of these things. Yet, these are entertainment, not strong sources of wisdom. *"A scorner seeks wisdom in vain; but knowledge is easy for one with understanding."* I let out a sigh. Do I remain the most learnèd at a party, or do I flatter my vanity (at the expense of today's topoi)? Is it not written:

"Tremble you weaklings / Cower in fear."

The Solune Prince - Chapter 10: The Aftermath of Thought; (or The N'Tariel Talent)

"Ah, hello Alexandre. You have not left?" Chloe sat down across from her.

Alexandre shook her head softly.

"Did you want a curriculum vitae?"

"A CV? Like a resume? No, I know about you from the professors I trade information with."

"A demo perhaps?"

"I, ah, don't think that...what is a demo?" Chloe knew the word, but not the context.

"A demonstration...of my ability as a researcher?"

"Oh, well, sure I guess. When?"

"Now." Alexandre's expression did not change.

"I don't, ah, I don't..." Chloe confused herself, "I don't think so."

"Then, let's go." She stood.

"Ah!" Chloe exhaled.

Alexandre Jutt smiled, and this time Chloe noticed that the woman's teeth were metal—a silvery metal. They looked heavy.

I wonder what happened?

They walked down Mash road, named because it was made not of cobble, but of mashed stone paste, hardened in the sun.

"I probably already told you this, but I study hormones. My research isn't much in demand, so I have not private funding," Said Alexandre.

"Oh. So who funds you?"

"The crown."

Chloe blushed, "I thought you did not want to work for the castle."

Alexandre's pale complexion brightened to match Chloe's. "So did I." She moved to change the topic.

"Most of it has been journal padding."

"Journal padding?" *I thought I knew all the academic jargon...*

"It's...padding the scientific journals. Adding—er, expanding on known ideas. Most of it is braindead or obvious, it rarely becomes useful unless someone is exhaustive about the process like Ar...A...Ari..." She physically grasped at air.

Chloe said, "Aristotle?"

"Sure. Anyway, aside from that there's one thing I'm working on in secret."

"Secret from even the crown?" Chloe gave an unpracticed, mischievous simile.

Alexander smiled back. "We have an arms-length relationship."

"Ah—"

"—But I guess you will find out soon enough."

"Oh!"

Chloe fidgeted, which made her almost trip. Alexandre caught her, by the neck and waist. "Err, sorry."

She let go.

"Ah, thanks..."

They made it to the Academy, and Alexandre led her to the Kemia building. Chloe looked at the school's bell tower clock. *It is nearly the eighth day-hour. So, two hours before dark. We should have time.*

They made it to Alexandre's office; a tiny room that Chloe assumed was once a supply closet.

"What, ah, what is this research then?"

Alexandre let them in and shut the door. It was black as pitch for a moment, and then Alexandre lit an oil lamp. She opened a drawer, extracted a notebook, and casually launched it at Chloe, who reflectively caught it.

They were standing in a sort of individual's lab. In fact, out of all the times Chloe had seen Alexandre, she had never looked as comfortable, as at home as she did when she entered the office.

Chloe opened the book and read the title on the first page. *Epinephrine*. She considered the word, surveying her brain for its meaning. She stared around the room. It was small enough that it likely couldn't fit more than three people; not comfortably, but it seemed to be fully equipped. There was an oven-sized blacktop (acid and burn proof) table in the centre, and a counter running along the far wall. *That, ah, Alexander's back cupboards are really tall...* There were two chairs leaning on the counter. On top of the counter, there were large metal cylinders marked "biohazard," as well as needles, tubes, measurement tools, a doublelens, and a cage with—"

"Animals?"

"Hmm?"

Chloe pointed.

"Oh," Alexandre mumbled, "Yeah, I borrowed some...rats."

"Why?"

"I'm trying to extract epinephrine—"

"Adrenaline!"

"—from them."

Chloe, excited to finally learn what she was here for, said, "So, do animals have the same sort of adrenaline as us?" She had a wild thought, "You're not running on rat adrenaline right now, are you?!"

"No! Eww! I haven't even successfully pulled from them yet! Eww! I'd be putting, oh my Con! Eww! What kind of weirdo are you to say something like that!"

Alexandre flushed.

Chloe shrugged. "What do you mean by pulled?" I thought I knew all the jargon, and yet, here comes Alexandre Jutt confusing me.

"Sorry, extracted. I kind of just say what makes sense."

"Ah...so what have you come up with?"

"Well, I've extracted adrenaline in fluids from myself, but uhg, these syringes are so heavy and stupid. I can't do anything complex or precise with them." She stopped, and thought.

Chloe said, "What about your secret!"

"Hmm. Well, it's really tiring, and I'm not consistent. Plus, it's...so numbing." Alexandre sighed.

"What! What is it!" Chloe did not like dancing around a subject.

"You know the talent of the East Metch? And the North Metch; the N'Tariel moreso?"

Chloe frowned, "And the...Elken?"

Jutt nodded. She stood straight and breathed. Nervously, she said, "Poke me or something."

"What?"

"I can't do it if I'm not stressed!" Alexandre yelled.

Chloe reached over the workdesk and poked Alexandre in the face.

"Your face is soft."

Alexandre frowned. She and Chloe locked eyes for a couple of minutes. Then, Chloe spoke.

She looked away and said, "I know someone who could do what you are attempting."

Alex sighed. "Solune Legend Salt Resz. Of course, he was N'Tariel. It's far easier for them."

Chloe said nothing. She studied the bits of paper and cardboard that littered the floor. She saw fabric poking out of one of the bottom cupboards.

"The Legendary Event was what inspired my research," Alexandre continued, "I've been in correspondence with an N'Tariel Æsthetician about this. Controlling their adrenaline is taught from a young age there, so for him, explaining it was like explaining basic maths..."

Chloe sighed, "It also comes more naturally to those of Metch descent. I have never seen someone who did not have that ancestry take control of their adrenaline to the degree necessary to evoke any meaningful change!" She was starting to heat up, and she didn't like it.

"What about the eldest prince Zealott? He claims to have achieved stable self-injected adrenaline rushes." Alex countered.

Chloe stepped away, hitting her back on the wall. "My brother?"

"Wait, I forgot—"

"What if he is just deluded? He is blonde, could you really tell the difference? He's been exiled for years! His words are never to be trusted!"

As Chloe spoke, Alexandre got an awful idea. She said, "What's so bad about this Zealott then?"

Chloe's eyes widened in rage. Her pupils opened; mydriasis. "Why do you think my sister left the kingdom? For fun? Abandon me? Nothing? Hate? Chase? Brother!"

Her words came out in abstract stream-of-consciousness. Alexandre rode the wave; she made a smug face.

What is she doing? "What is wrong with you?" Chloe said, "What are you trying to do?"

Alexandre Jutt's metallic-black smile widened, "Induce a stress response! You know I get anxious when I make social missteps!"

Alexandre Dirge exhaled sharp and her hair burst white.

"Ah!" Chloe tried to jump back, but she was already against the wall. She reflexively took up an unarmed marital pose.

"Ah!" She calmed, "You—you did it! Look at you!"

"Alexandre stood in place, her eyes darted around the room, just a little too fast. Chloe leaned in.

"Amazing, your hair has lost its colour. Look, ever your eyelashes, and" she looked Alexandre up and down, "even your body hair. Your almost glowing, Dirge!"

"I—I can't..." Alexandre burst out of the small office and turn around. Chloe followed.

"Let's spar. Come on, I saw that back there, you made a military pose, you're trained, aren't you?"

"Ah, my mother made sure of it; but here?"

Chloe looked around. The University hallways, with all its deep green floortiles, was empty, but it was only afternoon, so people were still there. Classes were in session.

"For research Chloe, come on. I have like seven more seconds."

"Seven seconds...six. Fine!" Chloe grounded her feet and leaned back. She threw a kick from the side, shooting her leg up and across, toes stiff. Chloe was four-and-a-fifth-cubits tall, 6.3 imperial feet, and a majority of it was legs. The strike hit light, a calibration. Chloe wound her calf all the way back. She immediately followed with another kick, in the same location.

Alexandre, taken off guard by the movement and confused by the first hit, was launched into the wall. Alexandre grabbed it and rolled to the ground, landing on one knee and launching herself to her feet.

She breathed, then ran beside Chloe, twice as fast as she should have, and threw a punch. It connected and, due to where Alex was standing, pushed deep into her opponent's gut. Chloe moved her hands inward to stop it far too late, but she kept going anyway to try and grab the arm. Alexandre pulled back and hit Chloe again, three times in a second; so fast Chloe saw only one blurred movement.

And then, Alexandre's hair faded back to normal, near-black. Chloe grabbed her with ease.

"I win!" She laughed. "Alex?"

The bell began to toll, the eighth hour of the day.

"Oh it's been so long since I heard the academy bell's toll." She listened to the sound, counting the hours. Then, she let go of Alexandre—or, she would have if the woman hadn't gone limp.

"Alex?" *She is unconscious.* "Ah, she said it was draining but...ah, wow."

Chloe pulled Alexandre into the room, laid her on the ground, and exited. She shut the door behind her. "Ah, I think that it will be nice having her in the party. I will, ah, I'll be right back."

Digression IIII - The Legendary Event: A Brief Account from Chloe Rhye

(Excerpt from The Solune Prince - Chapter 28: Walk the Earth Alone)

The Legendary Event was similar to a war, but it is technically to be seen as an invasion. An invasion of giants. They had come over the north wall and directly into Hannibal. They had come because they found the taste of the Solune to be pleasing to the highest degree. This event shocked the nation.

It shocked the nation because we had been expecting them, but we had been expecting something else. We were promised a grand deliverance. But ancient pacts had been fabrication all along, and promises had been perverted.

I had joined the battle back then, mostly to provide moral support to Janna, my sister. I was a year younger when it happened, but far less mature. Nothing worked out like we expected. Five of us, a small outer patrol, got pulled into the centre of the disintegrating city.

History records them as giants, but they were not. They were winged men who fought in white robes. They were the angels, but they were only a head taller than the Solune. But they had blank-looking eyes, and the disgusting teeth of carnivores. They had the strength of four men, but that the Creator we had four men for each one of them.

We kept up with the enemy for a while, staying alive and using the capabilities we had been accepted into the armies for possessing, but then one of them took Janna. She was grappled—she had seen allies fall like this; pulled into the enemy backline, ripped to the ground, and devoured alive—and so I moved. I sprinted past their frontline as she was pulled in, ripping my sword through an angelic ribcage and abandoning it in my pursuit. I was so far from her, but I still extended my fingers. I made my way past my confused enemies and leapt backwards over the ruined landscape and I screamed, with my eyes trained on my sisters determined captor.

And the feelings of my forefathers came over me. I heard the voices of the past. And when the fluids of my eyes began to drain down my face and mix with my tears, it felt so natural. They whispered from the days of my learning...

...For the king trusts in God, and in the mercy of the Most High; so that he will not falter. Your hand will suffice for to all Your enemies; Your right hand shall overtake those that hate You. You will make them as a fiery furnace at the time of Your anger; may God will consume them in His wrath, and let the fire devour them. Their fruit You will destroy from the earth, and their seed from among the children of men. For they intended evil against You, they imagined a scheme they cannot succeed in. For You shall make them a portion apart, You will make ready with your bowstrings against the face of them. Be exalted, Adonai, in Your strength; and will we sing and praise Your omnipotence.

— Account given by Chloe Rhye,
Three months after the opening of the walls.

The Prince annihilated every single one of the giants from the face of her kingdom.

It should here be noted that this was not an uncommon capability. In theory, anyone could learn to use the power of laszor eyes, though perhaps not with the Prince's degree of aptitude. This is similar in nature to the white-haired adrenaline rush of the northerners, which is accessible to the Riley, and to a lesser extend the Solune as well. While adrenaline comes more naturally to the N'Tariel, laszor eyes comes more naturally to the Solune.

Chloe, it seemed, had a natural talent. Typically, the rays of plasma come only from the eyes, but diving into enemy army had resulted in many wounds and abrasions. Chloe had unintentionally emitted from all of her open wounds.

The laszors chain-reacted with the minerals in the ground and magnified, as if through fission, erupting from the ground across the entire battlefield, firing skyward like house-sized jets of pale yellow light.

It discriminated, leaving Chloe's people untouched, and inundating the giants in a fury of chemical-like burns until there was nothing left but white bones. But Chloe, out of fear, never developed her laszor eyes afterward, and in fact it is rumoured she never used the ability again.

Span

Chapter 1: The Hunter.

When I was young, it was my mother who took care of me, but now I seem to be closer my father. It was because of him that I learned of my unusual nature. She taught me to walk, or so she tells me, and she was the one that informed my early actions. But, as I grew older, my father's frustration changed how it was our family functioned. Understandably, what he wanted was a pupil. He would talk about this, and about hunting over many afternoons.

When I was old enough, my mother began to teach me our domestic duties. I would clean the hearth, I would weave with her, and also, I would help her raise my younger sister. There were also duties for us to do outside the family. My mother and I would help around the tribe when people were sick, or needed their children taken care of, or needed to build something. The children, just like both of you, used to enjoy my stories. Well, I also liked to tell them.

I would talk about the forest, about the giant dogs, about the awful basket I once made that lost its bottom and dropped all of my fruits. But my favourite job was shearing animal skins, then cutting and eviscerating the meat. I volunteered for it often.

When my father's agitation began to spill into the family's afternoontime discussion, something within me was eager to hear about it. He would speak with frustration and wishfulness about his wanting to raise an apprentice; a hunter. He talked of this for many nights; in fact he went on all through the entire wet season. Maybe it was because of his problems that I became interested in hunting. I would ask him questions every afternoon. As I became more interested in his discussions, it seemed my mother did the opposite.

I was curious about difference the between the old hunting methods and the current ones, so I asked. My father explained to me how it was becoming far less common for a hunter to ambush—to grab his prey in his claws, but now they had better tools for the task. Then he sighed and began to talk about all of the things he could teach a son to do. It was at that time that he told us he would have liked to try to bear a son, but that he should not, that it was unwise. We did not have the resources for another child, he said. At that time, I did not understand what he meant. My mother did though, and seeing what this line of thought might lead to in the future, she told him to speak no more on that which he could not change. He said that her words were wise and so, to my dismay, he listened, and said no more of it.

I think it was because of this that I became a little troubled. The loss of the topic of hunting had struck me. Orin, you know her; well, after I had secluded myself for some days cleaning robbits and subjecting their corpses to my emotions, she came to me and asked what was wrong. I told her, and she said that it would be wise to talk to an a grandparent about my problems. She said that Sap would be a good person to ask. I waved my hand.

"My animal spirit is in a bad way. Speak not to me." I feel bad now for not thanking her.

It took me two or three days, I cannot remember, to build up the nerve to go speak to Sap. It was the first time that I had had to approach a man who was not my father. But, one day I finished early hanging the meat, so I took the short walk to his tent to see if we might speak. I heard shouts from inside. It was Sap and his wife. I thought about giving up and leaving. (Could you imagine?) He soon hobbled out of the tent and began to scream back through the door, but it was interrupted by a gag and then a convulsion. I thought that he was going to lose the food from inside him. He saw me and did what he deemed necessary to compose himself.

He said, "Why, then, child, are you here?"

I told him that I had become very unhappy because my father was unhappy. I said that he was longing for a son, someone to teach and apprentice, and also that I very much enjoyed and missed listening to his knowledges. I said that we would not have another child, and that my mother told him to stop speaking about things that he could not change. Sap laughed at me!

"What, Talc, who cuts our meat would like to kill it too? You must have an affinity for the dead." He considered me, suddenly looking serious.

I had never thought in this manner. It is good and right to be interested in what parents say; to take it into consideration, and so it had not thought about why I was so interested in my father's words. I agreed with Sap. He raised an eyebrow.

"You might be like Shell, girl," he said, waving his finger in an exaggerated fashion.

I squinted at the ancient man and then shrugged. We parted and I went to my mother to see if she had anything else I could help with. As I threaded an accent into a neighbour's new shirt, I thought of Sap's statement. I do not think that you know Shell, but I believe that her comparison to me was correct. In some ways. For a short time in her life she was a hunter. The more I thought about it, the more it made sense to me, the more my interest flared.

I asked my father about hunting again and he sighed, saying that Sandgrain's (awful name, he added,) son had been hunting since the beginning of the wet season and that he might go mad with jealousy. Mother spat at the ground, and my father shrugged at her.

I ignored them both, and said, "Would you like to teach someone to hunt then?"

He nodded slightly, and then glanced at my mother. She sighed and threw up a hand, resigning herself for the night. My father made an exaggerated frown and then looked back at me.

"Maybe I will be happier once I am grey like Sap and am too old to hunt. Then I can finally teach someone."

I swallowed my nerve and asked, "Why not teach me?"

There was a silence. My heart became the loudest thing at the circle, and I watched my father look around to my mother for an opinion. I was, after all, the child of both of them. My mother's expression shifted a few times; she was considering my words with severity.

"It does not matter to me! She is very slow at any task that is not cutting animals." At the insult, I looked at her, and she added, "You are also good with children as well."

And then, my poor sister dropped her soup, and my mother moved to help her. My father's expression was one of deep thought. He said finally, "Like old Shell then, blessed woman."

"What about Shell?"

"She and her second child died during her process. She had been a hunter in her youth, but she grew out of it with the coming of her first child."

"Oh."

He bared his teeth, "Tomorrow, you will have to wake up earlier than usual."

Span – Chapter 2: The Trapper.

Have you ever wondered why fathers sleep with their heads in a very specific spot in the house? I found out the reason that first morning, the morning of the day I became a hunter.

When the sun rises, its light fills the sky and drifts through the trees. It also drifts through the smokehole, and your father sleeps there, right where the light is brightest. Hunters are said by some to waken from the light. Everyone else awakes, as you know, to the elder's loud calls in the morning. But those who say light is the most reliable way, I now know, are incorrect. Now, I know better. The light is only a backup, for a true hunter awakens from the change of temperature a little before sunrise.

In my day, we were awakened by Sap, but now it is someone else, is it...it's grandmother. But on that day, I was awakened before the rest of the village by my father, because now I too was a hunter. My father put his hand on my head. My eyes opened and I looked around. He said with his eyes that I should remain quiet, and I followed him outside and towards the community pit. I watched my father's face as we went. It was flat; emotionless.

We were the second group to arrive. The man I knew to be Sandgrain, and his son, were there waiting. I didn't pay much attention to them, and neither did they to me. As people gathered though, I began to see eyes from the boys and the men. There were four kinds: anger, questioning, interest, and, of course, not looking at all. Sandgrain and his son fell into the fourth category. I counted and saw that everyone who should be there had arrived; our village had twelve hunters, not including me. Why weren't we leaving yet?

Someone, I think it was Silver, but I cannot recall, they said, "Where is that man!"

I tried to think of who might be missing. There were two possibilities, but only one face came to mind, and so too did that same face arrive at the circle of men.

"Of course yesterday was not so good. With that in mind, today we will be using the reliable methods," announced Sap, to many groans. He had arrived late, and it seemed that he was the one who kept stock of the hunts. He was the primary intermediary between the hunters and the village.

Sap looked at me and added, "Also, we have a new hunter. Today will be an easy day for everyone, so I don't expect that her apprenticeship will be too taxing. Ha!" he shouted, "Keep your vision on the animals, for the Terminal Spirit is always seeing! Talc, feel free to tell me or your father if anyone is getting on your nerves, yes child? No need to walk in Shell's footsteps and go beating on the poor young men." The elder laughed again. "Okay! Well! We all have hunting to do. The lesser spirits will take the hands that do not work, so let us be off before our limbs are no longer our own."

With that we dispersed. Everyone went to the storage building and took out a lot more gear than I was used to seeing hunters wear. Then my father and half of the men went northwest, and the other half went northeast. While I followed my father, he explained that this was not the usual way of hunting. The 'reliable methods' meant trapping. Today, he explained, they would be setting traps until the afternoon, and then checking them in the late evening.

"Reliable, yes," he explained, "but very boring, and it results only in robbits and other small catches."

As he spoke, I looked around to see who the others were. I recognised two; brothers who lived nearby. You know Silver and Quick? Well, this is how I met them. It seems their parents were trying to be clever; they were going to name their child after the chemia element, Mercury, and yet, it was decreed that there would be two and not one. Anyway, they, along with the others, sat on some of the forest rocks and began constructing things. They all worked with wood, straps, and string, and used our hands and stone knives.

"Watch here," my father motioned.

I watched as he constructed what he told me was a snare trap. He handed it to me, and gave me the same materials. He let me struggle to copy it while he proceeded to work on more.

"We will need a lot; they do not always catch something. No, you must wind it like this."

After a short period, Quick stood up. He already had a fistful of loops, and also held a bundle of thick sticks. He had made small notches in most of them, and had sharpened them on one end. Not long after, Silver and a few others finished as well. He and Quick said they would go ahead and look for good boulders. I asked my father what this meant, but he just said, "later."

After the second one, and a lot of help, I got a good handle on tying snares. By the time I had finished my fourth, though, he had made twelve. Then, he stood. This seemed to indicate readiness, but I didn't feel ready then. I looked up at him. He motioned with his head and we moved.

We were the second last pair to start down the footpath.

Span – Chapter 3: The Watcher.

"What is that?"

I pointed at the shape in the distance. It didn't look like anything I had cleaned in the past. My father peered between the trees, and crossed his eyebrows. He drew his spear—he had only brought one that day.

He whispered, "I have never seen such a creature. As a dog, but with long hair."

We watched it, and I thought at that time that it returned a gaze of its own. It moved, but my father and I were able to track it. It seemed to be too far for us to chase down; that is, if we went after it, it could easily run and hide long before we caught up.

"We will continue," my father said. He put his spear on his back and took one of the snares off of his shoulder.

He pointed, "See here is a good place, the trees are very close, and so they must go through this space. Hmm. Yes, this is so good; we will not need bait—now you tell me why."

This is how he spoke when he was teaching.

"I think..."

"No think, just look."

I looked at the spot. It was a small alley where two tree trunks crossed each other near their roots. Maybe I could have fit my fist in it. I looked around it, and confirmed that the brush was too tight everywhere else.

"This is a good spot, they have to go through there."

"Look."

I looked again, and then I saw it. Scratch marks in the ground, and claw marks in the wood.

"Oh," I said, "so this spot is already being used."

"We will not need bait." He handed me the snare. "Do not put your smell on it."

I set the trap, and then stood, looking around. "Where next—there again!" I whispered

I pointed this time, a foolish thing to do, and the creature saw me and hid. "What is that?"

"I do not know, I did not see."

We continued as if I had not seen anything. I set a few more snares. It was not hard to do. My father told me that I caught on faster than the boys did, I don't know if this was true. But, he told me that later he would teach me how to set the other sort of trap.

—

We reached the ridge around afterdawn. I was impressed by the sight.

"We are the village that is closest to the western ridge."

The cliff wasn't too deep; likely someone could climb it if they were skilled. Although, I would guess that if someone fell over, they would die twice over at least from the fall. At the base was a desert-like plain that stretched and expanded to the north. To the south was a stone wall, an artificial structure that still astounds me to this day. That is the Solune wall.

But I wasn't quite interested in either of those. I pointed straight ahead, and said, "What is that forest?"

My father sat down beside me and said, "That is no forest. If you went past that treeline, you would be shocked at how dark it is, it is always sunset there—it is always dusk in the Elken Yjungle. Look."

I saw what he meant. The trees were thick, and they looked to be only leafed trees, not a mix like here. "Who lives in the jungle?"

"The Elken people. They are our ancestors. One line in our heritage. Not a strong one, but a small and important part of our Great Root nonetheless. Later, I can tell you of them."

"Tonight?"

"Perhaps." He must have thought hard about it here. It was his night to speak at the community fire, and he wasn't sure if the Elken were a good topic.

—

We ran out of snares at the same time that we finally caught up with the rest of our party. Shortly after, the other half of the men arrived. I looked around at the clearing we had all gathered in, and saw the circle of rocks, the mounds and logs. This was a campsite!

"How was the woman, Errand?" Sandgrain called to my father.

"She catch on faster than your son, I would say," he laughed, "Lime, how long did it take you to learn to set a snare?"

"Eh," Lime looked between the two men, "three?"

I looked at my father. It seemed that he was unsure whether that meant three days, or three day fragments.

He said, "Talc can set a trap already. I will show her the deadfall on our way back."

Sandgrain looked impressed, but he did not voice it. He said, "You think she will mind her fingers?"

"We will see, I expect."

My father, Sandgrain, and Sour (the hunting elder at that time) gathered apart from the group to discuss. I saw that Silver and Quick were bickering in front of the pit, and snapping each other with leftover snare line. Lime and most of the other boys and men were gathering wood.

I figured I should be more useful than those who were sitting, so I went into the nearby brush to see what I could gather. There was not a lot of dead wood on the ground. I was unsure what to do. But you two know already of my capacity for cleverness! I looked around for a specific sort of tree, and started pulling at its branches.

After I had taken a few off, someone else saw me and called out a "Hey!"

I finished pulling and brandished my new stick. The boy sounded young, so I felt safe at this foolishness. He dropped all but the longest of his sticks and struck mine.

"You will never hit the target if you aim only at their weapon!" I said, swiping at his arm.

The attack hit, and he followed up, hitting me in the ribs. I thrust into his chest, and he fell over.

I said, "Maybe we should stop."

He coughed and looked up at me. He said, "You really are a girl, aren't you?"

I frowned, "I do hope so much."

"Do you really know how to set snares already?"

I realized that this was Lime, Sandgrain's son. "Yes, and I know when they do not need bait."

Lime stood up and leered at the ground. "I don't learn very fast," he said, "I'm surprised that you do, although, maybe that's normal, and I am just slow." He frowned. These were not his words, that is what I thought.

I did not like this manner of thought, especially not in a man-to-be. I said, "You will find no happiness if you only look at that which makes you unhappy."

He looked up at me. I added, "My grandmother says, do not speak of your flaws unless you intend to fix them and do not speak of your virtues except through your actions."

He said, "Oh," and began picking up his sticks. "Well, I came to say, you should get dry sticks off of the ground, and not take living ones from trees."

I decided to test his intelligence. I pointed to my tree and said, "Look."

He did, confused. After a minute the confusion wore off, and then he surveyed the ground. "Oh, that's a dead tree, is it?"

"Is mine not dry?"

"Huh. Okay."

Perhaps this boy was not so hopeless after all.

Inck

(Alice and Finch – Chapter 5: Negative Dawn)

Inck Alice Dawngale made her way through the dim snowy wood. She wasn't sure where to go. The south was barren. She would find no resources, no food there. She had survived on nothing but snow melted in hand for eight weeks, rationing the only food she had to her young child. For the most part, the child stayed on her back, wearing Inck's only shirt in addition to her own clothes to stay warm.

Inck had followed the base of the cliff west for two weeks, then east for six. She knew that she didn't have enough energy to double back again. She didn't have enough energy to continue much longer either. Her exposed shoulders were developing frostbite, her fingers spared only because she kept them crossed and beneath her arms. Trees stopped most of the winds, but Inck found little solace in this.

As she followed the cliff, the ridge had become higher and higher, and then suddenly it spiked. She was sidling a nearly vertical mountain at this point. On her back, the child Alice woke up. She slept a lot, lacking the energy to stay awake.

Inck said, "My Alice, my Alice, what shall we do? I've walked to the edge of my vision once then twice, but what I see remains the same. My legs will not take me beyond the naught I can see in front of us, east, west, or south."

"Ah, and we can't go that way right?" She pointed to the forest, "And we can't go back! So the only way to go is... north?" She pointed at the mountain.

Inck stared up the white spire. She could not tell for sure, but she doubted anyone lived at the top. She took her hands out of her armpits and stared at them. The Plainkind kept their clawlike fingernails long enough to be effective. In the past month and a half, they had continued to grow unbitten, unused.

Inck looked at the morning sky. She had a lot of time left, but she knew it still wouldn't be enough. She dug her fingers into the stone, satisfied that it was soft enough, and began to pull herself up, limb by limb, cubit by cubit. Alice watched from her back as they ascended in amazement.

Inck made it halfway up before her sleep reserves gave out. Her arms began to shake, her legs tremored. She paused for a moment.

Alice could feel the shaking, "Are you okay? Mum?"

"No. Just... Tell me about home." Maybe she could use a distraction.

"Home? The Plainkind Desert? It's warmer there. My dad is there. My friend, umm, Marisa. She's there too." Alice's voice was wistful, but still held onto its joy.

"And," Inck huffed, "What happened?"

"To get us here? Oh, well, we got lost in the sandstorm... We got stuck below the cliff. You tried to climb it, right? Yeah. It didn't, well it, yeah. It didn't, wasn't soft enough. So we tried to go around, both ways. It's cold down here. Snow is cool! But... Only for a while." Inck nodded, and started climbing again. Alice continued. "And now we're hungry all the time. And now we're climbing a mountain. And I haven't seen, we haven't seen anyone, anyone in long..." Alice got sad and so she stopped.

"It has been very long." Inck agreed.

Time passed as silence fell between them. Inck climbed, not looking back, her eyes ahead. The sun began to set, and soon night was upon them. Inck could see in the dark, but not as well with the cloud cover. She climbed primarily by feel. Some time in the night, she reached the top. In the dark, she could see that it plateaued.

"Ah."

Alice said nothing, asleep. Inck could see the opposite edge of the summit at the edge of her vision. She wasn't sure if she should rest or continue. She decided to continue. However, upon her first step, her exhaustion, her starvation, caught up with her. She felt contempt at her own condition, but she failed to stop herself from falling forward. She could not fall asleep yet.

There was only a veil of snow around them. Inck lay awake for the minutes required to melt it with her heat, and then she took her daughter from her back, and held her. Then she allowed herself to drift away.

She awoke before morning, a rest broken by bitter cold. She had another flash of her old life, a life of adolescent hunting, of eating. But now her life was doveoted to parenthood. She could not hunt, she could not eat, but mothering was something she could do. Inck positioned Alice on her back and started walking.

Her goal was to get to the other side of the mountain. Then she would be able to see all that lay to the north; to see where home was. Walking was far more difficult now. Her limbs ached and her stomach churned. Her legs still shook, and she had to pay attention or she might lose her balance.

Inck reached the other edge by dawn. She gazed out at the lush green lands in amazement. The sun's war rays woke Alice, and she saw it too. "Wah! Look!"

Inck nodded. She pointed. "There is our home to the northeast. In front of us is the walled Solune Kingdom. And look, another group of settlements lies to the northeast."

"All we have to do is get down!" Alice was excited.

Inck doubted that she had the energy to make the climb down. Her reserves were at their limit, and there was no food on the mountaintop.

A frightening solution came to her as she looked down at the plummet. A Plainkind's body could survive such a landing. The injuries would undoubtedly be her undoing, but she would have the strength to protect her child from the inertia first. She put the thought aside for the moment.

Inck dug into the ground for a couple of stones. She was familiar with rocks and found two, a softer and harder stone. She copied something in the Plainkind script and then began to climb down. On her back, Alice excitedly twisted around, looking at the world below. She wanted to go back home, but was also interested in this new kingdom.

This descent was the most difficult thing Inck had done. She could feel her muscles giving way. She wondered if they could do such a thing. As they went further, Alice became more and more worried about the shaking.

One-third of the way down, Inck had to stop. She steadied herself. Aside from her tremors, she could not move. Physically she could not continue. She looked down and wished upon her ancestors that she'd had the strength to continue just a little further. Inck closed her eyes. She wished she hadn't headed west for so long. She held onto the regret for only a moment.

Then she thought of Alice, who must have been concerned, clinging to her back. Inck knew that one of them would survive the fall. She channelled her life – her reserves. She shed her regrets. And then, she pushed away from the mountain.

Alice screamed out in shock. She couldn't understan what was happening. She clung to her mother as tightly as her small body let her. It was tight enough. The fall ended sooner than expected, and Inck took the landing as hard as she could. Nearly all the force went into her leg muscles, and then into her bones. Her shins and thighs crumpled under the force. Most of her vertebrae fractured. Her daughter felt the force of multiple gravities, but was unhurt overall. She dropped off her mother's back and ran around to her front.

"Mum!" She looked at her mother with a pleading expression.

"Dear Alice... Alice May Dawngale..."

Inck looked at her lower half, damaged beyond conventional healing. She watched blood ooze slower and slower as her outer wounds healed superficial. Still she did not let go.

She said, "When I stop moving, wait but a day. Then, bury me in front of that boulder."

Inck pointed with her long damaged fingernail. It must have been part of the mountain at some point because it stood out in contrast from the surrounding forest.

"Copy this onto it."

She handed the stone to Alice. Alice could not read it. She couldn't read anything yet.

I am your Mother, Inck Alice Dawngale.

They spoke together, of home, of Alice's father who had lost the rest of his family to the sea of sand, the sandstorm, and their perilous journey. But Inck spoke primarily of Alice's future.

"You must find a home for yourself, even if it is not our old home, if it is with the Solune. You must live a good life for yourself, for me." Inck shed a deep iron-red tear.

Alice nodded, and embraced the parts of her mother that were still alive. She too cried tears of ruby. Though it was only morning, the two, exhausted, slept together for the last time.

Alice awoke the next evening, and felt her mother. She was warm, but it seemed to Alice not to be the warmth of life. Alice scavenged for food and found many strange fruits. She returned and fed some to the mouth of her mother.

"..." Inck exhaled and gave Alice one final look, a look of hope. And then she died.

Alice looked at Inck for a long time, frozen, staring at the vacant expression of hope for many moments. And then, when she felt she had absorbed all she could from Inck's last mortal message, when she had taken in the final emotion from her mother, Alice moved. She reached forward and closed her mother's eyes. She took the unknown fruit and ate it.

Then she began to dig.

Kēmeía

"I found this behind the bar." Setzer handed Natasha a thumb-sized glass vial. It was empty, but lined with a distinct maroon residue. "They must have been poisoned."

"Yes," said Jade, "There was something wrong with the taste."

For the first time since the inn had been built, there was more than one person in its attic. Three of those seven were dead.

Setzer didn't like the involvement of Jade Sing. He disliked her for a lot of reasons. Jade was an unusual foreigner, and worse, she was a cannibal. Natasha didn't seem to be interested in arresting Jade, despite Setzer's suspicions. Every time he'd investigated one of Jade's catches, she had come away innocent. Did she eat people? Yes. But did she kill them? Not according to the evidence. Cannibalism wasn't technically illegal, and so it appeared that Jade simply took advantage of other people's murders. She was a clever opportunist. Jade had broken into the inn attracted by the scent. She had found the bodies and apparently sampled them. Then she had alerted the nearest guard, Sergeant Alice;  a small, jumpy woman built like a brick wall. Alice told Natasha, the towering, stoic, guard Captain, and they had both arrived along with Constable Setzer, a short, often cross young man with long black hair, pale skin, and dark eyes.

To Setzer's chagrin, it seemed he was again going to prove Jade's innocence. He surveyed the corpses. Each was missing part of its calf, and one's face was so bludgeoned that it was unrecognisable.

"Wonderful!" Alice clapped. "Easy to draw a conclusion based on this," he said. "First, based on the vial and the... taste, we can assume that these people were poisoned. Second, Dhesmond Machina owns and runs this inn. He could easily spike his alcohol and claim that the victim passed out. Finally, the inn didn't open today, and," he handed Natasha a copied document, "yesterday's travel ledger shows he skipped town and hasn't returned!"

Natasha studied the list and felt her neck tighten.

"Good job, but this is not enough."

"Okay..." Setzer said, "what else do I need?"

She looked at him calmly, "Who are these people? Where did the poison come from?"

Setzer wasn't happy, but orders were orders. "Fine, we'll identify the bodies first."

"Good." Natasha's face was stern, "After you two are finished, meet me at the Ph.Ch. lab. Alice, I would like you to visit the undertaker for this area and get them to identify the body, whether you identify it or not. If the district mortician can identify it quickly, bring us a note, otherwise, come without it."

"Sure," Alice nodded

Setzer sighed. "Alice, do you know who usually comes here?"

"I know almost just about all the people from around here." Alice's grasp of syntax faltered when she was excited.

Natasha left them and exited the building, studying the ledger. She surveyed the cobbled streets, and then headed northwest to speak to one of the city's construction foreman.

Setzer and Alice sat at a table in the bar and drew up a list of all the patrons. Alice identified the two who were dead, and they crossed them off. Then Setzer went out into the city and sought out the rest of the list. Jade stayed behind, tasked with keeping people out of the bar. After much frustration, he had bargained her into promising that she would "try not to eat anything," and "definitely not touch the mysterious body." He hoped he wouldn't have to answer to families again.

It took until noon to find everyone on Alice's list. Most of them wondered why the bar was closed. One person mentioned that Dhesmond had become too touchy. Most of the other patrons agreed that, in the past month or so, he had seemed more stressed than usual. Setzer and Alice thanked each person for their time, and soon the list was empty, except for one name.

Alice looked, and shook her head, "Reighleigh Straker. We only checked his house, remember? He's maybe at work."

It dawned on Setzer why the Captain wanted them to meet her at the lab. "Does he work at the Ph.Ch. lab?"

"Yep."

"Natasha must have known all along... Now we just have to confirm that he isn't there and our bases will be covered." Setzer nodded to himself.

Alice just shrugged, "We'll meet there after I go to the cemetery."

"I doubt we'll need it, but orders are orders, I guess."

To his surprise, Setzer arrived first and had to wait a few minutes. Natasha arrived with the slight sheen of a person who just walked halfway across a city and back.

"Where did you go?" asked Setzer.

"I went to where they are extending the wall."

"Oh."

"Did you find the identity of the third body?"

"Reighleigh Straker. Not sure why Dhesmond would beat him up like that though."

The Captain shook her head.

"You will see when we go inside the Philosophy of Chemia Laboratory," She returned the vial he'd found at the inn. "Search his desk."

Natasha knocked on the door. It was answered by a woman who looked like her, except she was younger, smaller, wore a white coat, and had more hair.

"Natasha?" She asked.

"Chloe," she nodded. "We are here as part of an investigation."

"Ah, sure. I'll get someone who actually works here." She turned and called, "Straker?"

Setzer glanced at Natasha. If Reighleigh was here, alive, then his investigation was worthless. A moment passed, and she called out again, but for someone else.

"Finch? Yes, ah, the guard is here."

Chloe let them into the lab. It was brightly lit, with large wooden desks. Some were capped with thick layers of metal, but all of them were covered with instruments and lined with drawers. In the far corner was a small room sealed with a heavy door.

Finch approached them. He was a short man with pale skin, dark hair, and dark eyes. He wore a white lab coat and held a mess of papers.

"Oh, Captain Rhye," he looked from Natasha to Chloe, "Here to talk to your sister?"

"No. We speak when we are not working."

Setzer said, "Is Reighleigh here? I need to—" see if he's alive, is what he thought. "I need to search his desk."

"He's in the supply locker right now." Finch pointed, "It's heavily barred to prevent theft. Some of that stuff is dangerous."

There was a loud metallic creak and Setzer's stomach churned. According to his deduction, the man who stood before them was dead, his body stashed in Dhesmond's inn. He took a deep breath. He hadn't earned the rank of Constable through faltering. He defaulted to his orders.

"We are here to search your desk."

Reighleigh gave him a deep frown.

After a pause, Finch pointed to one of the counters, "It's that one."

Setzer strode to it and began opening drawers until he found one filled with thumb-sized test tubes, and a labelled jar of distinct red liquid. He took out the vial from the inn. Its size and shape matched, and the colour was the same.

Natasha stood with Reighleigh and Finch on one side and Chloe on the other. She looked sidelong at the doctor. He seemed to be stifling his nerves. She watched his hands and saw that his knuckles were blue.

Setzer read the label on the jar, Hyperthermic Coronary Accelerator and then looked up and nodded to Natasha. She nodded back. They'd found the poison supply.

Then Alice flung the front door open, and jumped inside.

"I got it!—Oh, hi Finch—anyway, I got it!" She waved the mortician's note in front of her, "The last dead person is not Reigh even for sure now, it's Dhesmond Machina!"

Reighleigh's face hardened. He sprinted to the door. Alice smiled and repositioned slightly. Reighleigh tried to tackle her, but unfortunately for him, Sergeant Alice was nearly twice his weight in muscle; a capable guard in the occupational sense well as the literal one. She easily restrained him.

"You're under detainment for killing three people using this poison!" Setzer ran to the man and seized his hands. he began winding a cord around Reighleigh's wrists.

The man retorted, "How could I have murdered someone who isn't even in town!"

"You—" Setzer had no idea.

Natasha finally spoke, "You followed him, but not through the gate. You went through the part of the wall that is under construction."

Setzer and Alice looked at each other across the man who stood between them. Reighleigh remained silent.

Finch was unsure what to think.

Chloe called out, "go on!"

Natasha strode to the nearest desk and sat down.

She faced Reighliegh, "Jade confirmed for us that all three of the victims were poisoned. The liquid and vial found at the inn match with the poison and containers found here. Likely they were killed under your instruction, using your chemical."

Setzer had finished, so he presented the items Natasha mentioned.

"Shortly before we came here, I confirmed that, on the same day that Dhesmond left, the foreman saw him return through her construction site, along with someone else; you. I assume you exited before the workday started and managed to convince the poor back. Then you poisoned him like you did everyone else; except he would have known his fate when you handed it to him.

"You threw Dhesmond's body with the rest. But," Natasha pointed to his bruised hands, "you beat the recognition off his face first."

She took the ledger, and dropped it beside her. "You left Dhesmond's closet full of skeletons, with his name on a document proving that he left town. You framed a dead man. It would have been the perfect crime—if there was no one who could identify a dead body. But there is, and dead men do not sneak into cities or poison and brutalize themselves."

The Solune Prince – Chapter [unknown]: Projection Exercise

Taking a pre-existing novel, and projecting far ahead of the present writing location, and writing a chapter there.

1

It was, yesterday. We were spraying, as usual. I admit we were spray painting. Look, I know the law and we had the permits. Show them the permits. We had the right to be there.

If I were less ethical, I could have blamed the other guys. In fact, I could have abandoned them and ran. But I am a man of Noah, and I know the law; at least I know that part. This happens a lot. Police usually don't know anything, they just don't. Luckily for us, I do.

'Hey! You can't be markin' up that wall like that! Is that another one of them canted x-shape? It's you lot then, markin' up the town! You best give all that up and come in with us.'

I heard them shouting, so I came, I ran. But, man, my peers are so...so good at fumbling up tense situations. Good thing I know the urban sprint. Hop, skip, run up the walls, onto the trash, swing off the window bars, slide down the side, skid 'round the corner, man. Nice.

"You best leave my team alone. We're here on business." That's what I said. Business. Usually stops them. But they didn't even hear! Looks like the 'prince' over there already had it down, but damn! She was talking the wrong law! Where is she from?

She said, 'No, this isn't public property, it's without your jurisdiction unless you get a formal complaint. Look, he has our papers, this is a job. What about you? Do you have your papers? Was there a complaint? Any warrant for you being here?"

Oh man, that's not how things work here missy! After that, well, whew, violence man. We didn't even move, but missy dismantled everyone for us. No sweat.

2

The litigator moved on to a different witness. "And you, you were there, my lord?"

'As a bystander. I only saw the second part.'

"Please describe what you saw."

'Haha. Missy, that's miss Chloe Rhye, fifth Prince of the Solune. They don't have the honorific "princess" where she comes from. What a people, the Solune. She dismantled your three officers in seconds. Truly admirable—from a tactical perspective.

'The draw of her weapon became the first attack, a cut across the chestplate of your first man. She flicked back the instant she'd made her hit; truly, a trained movement. Her weapon was back out before it could be seized—she slid into tierce with little effort.'

"Could you please limit the technical—"

'That's a point-up guard. She followed tierce up with a four, and then another four—'

"Please, the—"

'—That's an underhand thrust that ends in an upward sweep. Your men are so slow that she could hit with four twice before having to go back into a carte. And Chloe didn't even bother moving onto the later cycles, although maybe she doesn't know them. Regardless, she held carte and just kicked the poor man to the ground.

'The rest fell likewise; engage stance on the secondary officer, (she has a terrific engage), into a one, into prime parry stance, smack the tertiary officer with a two, up to…I really wish she would protect her sword arm, but no, she slides back into engage carte, beats the secondary officer's pikesword out of his hand, a smack to the face with the off hand, and then, no guard whatsoever, she grips her sabre two-hand (a very bad idea), and hits an oncoming attack from the tertiary. And then, lo! Kicks officer three to the ground as well! To my great pleasure, she cycled back to a carte, and then a prime hanging guard before sheathing. You may now understand why it is she prefers the military sabre to the officer's one.'

"…You seem almost pleased about this."

'Truly; I trained her in the sabre.' At this, the first witness laughed. 'Further, as royal emissary, Prince Rhye, I believe, is subject to diplomatic immunity. Why she was with these vagrants is beyond my knowledge, however, she should answer to the Lussa royalty, not the law. I assume that you have contacted Prince Ryann?'

There was a short discussion among the court, and then recess was called.

Raze

When she had finished speaking, she stared at me.
Her look was unusually intense.
I looked at her rather intensely, wiping my mouth.
She wiped her mouth, glaring at me openly.
Perhaps she lacked a sense of etiquette, or perhaps the intensity came from an underlying edge—perhaps more than an edge—of...something.
"And as a result," I continued, "I'm now in control of our group." I think I spoke too loudly. Hopefully she will just think I'm nervous...
She was rather loud, but she didn't seem nervous. There was something disconcerting about this woman. She had black, shoulder-length hair. Her skin was unhealthy, pale, and her eyes had the intensity of sleep deprivation. "You are telling me that you have taken control of the **Caironea gang**?"
"The...Alexandre gang now." I think I spoke too loudly. STOPISHOULDSPEAKONLYWHATISNECESSARY
I noticed something strange about her mouth.
"You said your name was Alexandre Dirge."
IVERUINEDITRUINEDI I couldn't tell if she had asked me a question or if she had simply made a statement. IRUNIEDIRUINEDDONTTELLALLJUST LETHERLOCKYOUAWAYAND
When I had received her letter, I was certain that it would lead either to some sort of attack, or perhaps a joke. Yet here I am not fighting. Further, those who play tricks do not typically also confess murder to the Captain of the Guard. I felt that I had heard the name before...Dirge.
"I may have a proposition for you. I should arrest you; however my operation would be undermined if, through justice, you were detained. For this reason, I will trust you to return here again, tomorrow. At the same time."
LOOKATWHATYOUVEDONE I looked at her rather intensely. I waited a moment. I took a few breaths, and then I opened my mouth to speak. "—"
"This does not mean that you will escape the law, however..." I was in no position to, on my own, make promises; but I needed to entice her return. "You may be able to make partial atonement if you aid the Kingdom."

I closed my mouth then winced. I wondered what she had in mind. When I confessed, I had been hoping this would be it, that all this would be over.

I saw her wince. I also saw her mouth properly, saw her teeth. This woman had a full mouth of broken—seemingly violently, perhaps even purposefully—broken teeth.

I assumed that meeting with the Captain of the guard herself, meeting with Natasha Rhye, would guarantee my arrest, but it seems that I'll...have to return tomorrow ANDLOOKATHOWIFAILMYSELFIFAILMYSELFEVERYTIMEIFAIL I took a breath. My eyes focused on the city wall behind her, and then it came back to me; and what had put me in this situation in the first place. OHNOWHATHAVEIDONEIVEFORGOTTENMYOHNOOHGODOHHOW COULDIFORGETMYOWN......

"Partial atonement if I aid the Kingdom..." HOWCOULDIWHATHAVEI-DONEWHATHAVEIOHNOWILLIBE

I could see it in her face again, that edge of...madness perhaps. It seemed to have heightened. I said, "I can rely on your return, then?"

IBEABLETOFULFILLMYORIGINALINTENTIONHOWCOULDIHAVEFOR-GOTTENMYOWN "Yes, I will return." I made the mistake of giving a courtesy smile. I realized, and quickly covered my teeth.

I confirmed my observations on her mouth. I had thought that there was something disconcerting about her, but perhaps it was her situation. Or perhaps both are the case.

FORGOTTENMYOWNWHATISWHATISTOCOMEWHATISTOCOME
Morning was coming. I could see the light.

X X X

I took the day to do research, in addition, obviously, to my job. I spoke to some of my own guards, then to Vinth, the Captain of the Castle guard, and then gave up on receiving any information of use. Though; my guard, Finch Dirge Zeth, informed me that his mother's name was Diesel Dirge. I did not ask about Alexandre, though perhaps there is some relation. Captain Vinth, too, had some information about a Hail Dirge in the underground gang, but I did not believe her to be the Dirge I sought.

I next spoke to the Solune Agent, Janna Rhye; my sister. The agents knew of the Dirges. There was a Dirge already running a gang: Diesel Dirge, she whose group occasionally raided the neighbouring town. There was also another Dirge, in another group. I assumed that this was Hail. Janna said there were three gangs: Diesel, across the Kingdom; Caironea, to the north east; and Horith, underground in Murdock, my city.

Perhaps the young Dirge was not lying.

ASINGLECHILDISLIKEASINGLEPARENTUSELESSANDDAMAGEDANDYETMOTHER IS THIS NOT US? AND WHY? WHO IS TO BLAME? And I had forgotten...

X X X

"Are you willing to take on this task? The gua—"

"Yes. I will take on your task."

She must have some motive, though why she was so willing when there was, possibly, family in neighbouring groups, I was not sure.

WHOISTOBLAMEWHOISTO And now, it seems we have been rewarded with providence, mother. CANYOUSEE this is a divine gift? The deal will help us.

"When should we take on this...operation?"

"I could have the guard ready in two days."

WHATNONONONONOICANTDOTHATICANTGOTHATFASTTHATSRIDICULOUSNOTEVERYONEISASEFFICIENTASYOUARERHYE "I...cannot."

"Of course. If you only just took control of the gang, then you will need to gain at least some semblance of trust from them. Right now there is something else I need from you."

GAINTHEIRTRUSTENOUGHTHATTHEYWOULDFOLLOWMEINTO

"I will put it very simply. First, the guard will help with the operation. You must initiate, but we will provide the motivation. Then, of course, we will aid with clean-up. That is first. Second, I need evidence. This is to be a large operation. Three parties will be involved. I need evidence of your words that Caironea is truly dead. Finally, you need to send your gang on some sort of small mission to prove to them that you are capable."

"That's only two," GAINTHEIRTRUSTGA "because the way I'm going to... —The task I have in mind is the public shaming of the body. We will take it and abandon it outside the city gates." I looked at her rather intensely, and pointed past her to the walls that loomed behind us.

Perhaps it was madness indeed. I did not think too deeply on it. If this woman could coordinate a gang of fighting men in this task, she would certainly be capable of the rest. We agreed to meet again in exactly one week.

X X X

We worked for six days. By the sixth, the group had enough confidence in me to perform the task.

We dragged the body to the city gates and dumped it. Propped him up against the doors. Someone wanted to pin the corpse with stakes through the shoulders, to nail him up, but we were spotted. The guard does their job, it seems. WERANAND on the seventh day we rested, and I met with Natasha.

"I made sure the guards saw you, to heighten the experience. Should the operation succeed, your term will likely be greatly shortened." Especially if, as I suspect, you acted in self-defence...and who did you kill but a known criminal?

WEARESOCLOSESOCLOSESOCLOSEMOTHERSO "When is it?" **CLOSESO**

"Two days."

I covered my smile.

"Before we part, you must tell me Horith's location. Then, I will tell you how our end of the operation will function."

X X X

True to her word, the Captain provided motivation. **ANDAPPARENTLYSOMEOFUSHAVEACONSCIENCE** A member of Horith's gang, a man named Vinth, brought news from within the city.

Perhaps there is something—fortune, I suppose—on that young woman's side. We did not need to create a scenario by force, rather, our undercover guard Vinth had something for us. Horith's gang was intent on expanding and overthrowing first the Alexandre gang, in its perceived newfound weakness, and then later the Diesel gang. Monopoly over independents. Vinth simply played the part of a concerned neighbouring member.

"We will take them pre-emptively," was responded to with mostly cheers. It seems my past mistakes as a tactician were either forgotten or...were not as grand as the corporal punishment I received for them would suggest. I tried to clench my teeth, felt pain, gave up, and then began to assemble a plan. That had been my task before all of this **FAILURE** had occurred.

X X X

Lined pockets. We broke the windows shortly after beating the door in. We moved in headfirst; me first. It seems our architecture of aggression comes into reality faster than theirs. We caught them unaware, men at the boardroom table. I commanded the assault, rocks streamed out, beating flesh, and then swords were drawn. I commanded the rest to other parts of the building, and then I moved ahead.

The controlled chaos, organized mess, took to the background as I skulked the building, searching. The noise was all finally on the outside of my mind. Through the roar of dissent, I heard a saccharine laugh. I drew my sword and opened the door.

We had watched them fill their pockets with stones and then storm through the front. Then I told my guard to wait until it became loud, and then wait a few more seconds. We would fall upon them when they were weakened.

"You did this, didn't you." He had her by the neck. "**That daughter of yours, you told her!**"

Horith had made the mistake of trying to intimidate her. At the point of death, Hail Dirge had a habit of...laughter. "How wonderful I must be, how powerful, to have the ability to be in two places at once!" She giggled.

He turned in time to receive a cut across his face. His eyes widened, which I took as permission to drive my fist into his throat. I kicked him to the ground and smiled openly. "In the middle of a siege, your first instinct is to find someone to blame. Oh..." I put my foot on his chest, and then looked around, "Do you hear that? Listen. The guard is here."

The Solune Guards is trained and skilled. Our weapons, seemingly simple rods of steel, beat past the swords most criminals choose to carry and keep us committed to blunt force instead of blood.

"Everyone who survives—which should be most of them—is to be run through the courts." We poured in, interrupted the partially-completed battles and began, with ease, to finish them on both sides' behalf.

"No, mother you have to go!"

She said, "Where?"

"Out." I pointed to the window, breaking and clearing it with my sword. She looked at me with deep apprehension. Reading my face, she gave a tragic smile and then...laughed. She leaned in close to my face and whispered, "I'll see you some other time then. And...take care of yourself my dear."

I nodded, we said goodbye to each other, and then she climbed stupidly out the window.

Shortly after, Captain Rhye appeared at the open doorway.

Mariça

Forced change; the result of avoidance.

1

Marisa wandered around the sands near the northern mountains. She knew the Shriken, those people who could fly, lived there, and maybe she would run into one. She looked up the mountain, and then further into the sky. It was getting dark, so she decided to return to the village.

"Marisa, what did you catch?" Jan asked, "Yaska's hunt wasn't very big today, it might not be enough."

Marisa frowned. "Ah well, I forgot about that. I explored."

Jan's smile faltered. He said, "Well, next time keep the exploring for afterward." He smiled again, "let's see how far we can stretch what we have."

—

It came up again at supper. First, the children were fed and then everyone else split what was left. It was a little less than usual.

Yaska said, "Marisa, this village has become large again. That is why you were trained to be our second hunter. I know that you have been doing it alone for only a few weeks, but if you do not attend your duties, you will continue to bring home nothing."

Marisa finished her food and then stared into the fire.

"Marisa, if you continue to neglect, we will find a new hunter. Jan will have to take your place in the meantime. He trained me. Or maybe you just need some re-training?"

"No I don't need that. Don't worry about it."

—

The next day, Marisa went out hunting once again. She took her dart, the Plainkind throwing sword, and headed north, searching the desert for prey. She hoped to see one of the dinosaurs that Plainkind preferred to feed on.

As time passed and she surveyed the plains, Marisa allowed herself to wander further and further north, her route wilfully deviating towards the mountains.

"I've been searching for quite a while, I will take a break." She walked along the base curiously, and reached a cave she had never noticed before. "Of course, taking a break in the shade is a good idea," she sang.

So Marisa stepped into the cave and sat down on a portion of the ground. She ate a bit of dried meat and looked around. The cave split off in many directions.

"I wonder if these lead anywhere, or if they just end."

Scanning her eyes, as if looking for prey, Marisa saw a sparse but suspicious trail of sand heading down one of the tunnels. She considered returning to explore it later, after she had gotten food for the village, but she convinced herself that the trail might be disturbed or that she may never find this cave again. So, she reasoned, she must explore the cave immediately. Standing up, she followed the sand trail into the cave. After moving inwards a little ways, the tunnel opened up into a small cavern that was dimly lit by sunlight streaming in from a hole in one of the walls. Opposite from her, Marisa saw engravings. She saw, drawn into the walls, three simplified people.

Marisa clapped her hands together, "How exciting that now I may find something! I knew that exploring wasn't useless. Now!" she clasped her hands together, expectantly, "What meaning does this have for me?"

Marisa studied the engravings. The first person looked to be a Plainkind person. The skin was hatched to look darker, the hair black. The form was stout and strong. Then, the last one looked the same, but had giant wings. That must be a Shriken. In between the two symbols was a foreign and fearsome creature.

"It looks like a larger Plainkind that hasn't taken care of herself," Marisa mused. "These lines coming from the hands, are they nails? And this hair, it's long and wild. I have never seen anyone like this." She looked between the three images, and then at the lines scrawled between them. She traced them with her finger, thinking. "I wonder...is this—are these stages perhaps? Plainkind, then this in-between creature, and then—"

"A Shriken."

The voice echoed across the cavern and Marisa's hairs stood on end. She turned around and saw a woman standing in doorway. She was no taller than herself, but she was older, and had large, leathery wings folded behind her back. She also looked much stronger.

She asked, "Who are you?"

"I'm Marisa."

"No, no, you are a Plainkind, you should not be here. And you saw this, you understood it. No, you should not be here!"

Marisa watched the Shriken woman's face. She looked angry, but also something else. Was that worry.

"If you know about the cycle, then you cannot leave."

2

Even though her skin wasn't very loose or wrinkled, it was tanned and greyed. It was thick, and behind it were layers of muscles; so many muscles that Marisa wondered if she had extras that the Plainkind did not. Her hair was thick and black, but clean and brushed. Marisa was jealous.

The Shriken took a step forward, and Marisa ripped the hunting sword from the clasp on her back and pointed it straight forward. She had only ever used her sword against wild animals. She wasn't sure if she could fight a skilled opponent.

The Shriken sighed and then leaped forward. In an instant she was in front of Marisa, as if she had teleported. Her arm swung low, into the girl's stomach. Marisa fell to the ground coughing. She felt a foot on her back, and then the Shriken woman spoke.

"I don't know what to do with you," she sounded uneasy, "but I cannot let you go. I will take you to the rest of the council."

The Shriken stood Marisa up and grabbed her by the shoulder. Marisa held tight to her sword with the other hand as she was led back out through the cave. When they got to the entrance, Marisa pulled her arm upwards and swung at her captor.

The Shriken stopped the attack at the wrist and wrenched the sword from Marisa's hand, throwing it onto the stone ground and stomping on it. She looked Marisa in the eyes as she bent the weapon into a groove in the floor.

"If you do not struggle, I will not hurt you."

Marisa looked at her defiantly. It was all she had left. She was lead out of the cave and towards the neighbouring mountain. She looked into the sky. The sun was getting low, she should be returning soon, and returning with food, but she wasn't sure if she'd be able to now.

Marisa was led into another, more hidden cave. After a short journey into the mountain, the cave opened up. The walls were smooth and the ceilings cavernous. It was dark, but Marisa found her eyes adjusting.

She was led into a smaller room with a round table. There were three other male Shriken, two were sitting, one with light hair, the other with dark. Seeing them up close, Marisa realized how similar they looked to the Plainkind. Stronger, aged, maybe a bit taller, and winged, but other than that quite similar. They looked up.

"What is this Plainkind doing here, Jolanin?" The man with dark hair asked.

"She was in one of the caves," said the Shriken, Jolanin.

The light haired one said, "Which cave?"

Jolanin said, "The one with the life cycle in it. It was not sealed, and she got in."

He stood and told the Shriken that was not at the table, "Seal that part of the cave." Then he turned back to Jolanin, his face tense, "Take the Plainkind you found. Bar her in an extra room for now. We will have to figure out what to do."

—

Marisa was put into a small bedroom. Her captor, Jolanin, said, "I am going to seal you in here until we come to a decision. We do not often have issues like this, so it may take some days."

"Days!" Marisa said, "Days? You can't keep me here for days!"

"I will see what I can do for you, but the rest of the council will likely be slow to decide." Jolanin pointed to the bed. "You can use that." With that Jolanin exited the room and closed the door. Marisa followed and pushed on it. She figured out how to work the door latch and tried it, but, as she assumed, nothing worked.

"This is stupid. What do they want me to do? Why is the life cycle so important anyway? So what if I know that Plainkind can become Shriken? Gah!"

She gave the stone door one last kick, and again nothing happened.

—

Yaska had a successful hunt, and then had finished her day quite early. When, by supper time, she did not see Marisa return she figured that the girl was either neglecting her duties again or was having troubles. When nightfall came, she became worried.

In the dark, she discussed with Jan. "I should search for her."

Jan said, "Well, she has come back later than this before. There might be nothing to worry about."

"Fine," Yaska said, "but if she is not here tomorrow, you will be hunting, because I will be searching for her."

Jan shrugged, and the village went to sleep.

—

Marisa, tired of resentfully pacing the room, eventually did use the bed, and as the night went on, she began to dream.

She was hunting dinosaurs. She really wanted to finally kill one and get Yaska and Jan off her back. She had the strangest feeling that the dinosaurs were everywhere except where she was looking. She scanned the desert to the left, and they ran to the left just outside her eyesight to avoid her gaze. She scanned right and, predicting her, they moved right. She just couldn't see. Then she felt a person beside her. It was a woman, and she led Marisa into the cave.

The woman said, "I am Death. Or rather, I am the Servant of the phenomena death."

Marisa didn't know what to say, what to feel. She said, "Am I going to die, because I saw this cave?"

Death said, "Something like that. Probably anyway."

Marisa looked at her. She had long black hair and pale skin. She was dressed in dead furs that were cured and tanned, cut thin and blackened. She looked studious and orderly, but she wore a playfully devious expression. Was this really Death? She seemed unfitting in Marisa's eyes.

"Wait, why probably? Don't you know if someone's going to die?"

Death shrugged, "I have access to more information, variables whatever, but I don't know the future. I'm not the Servant of Tendrils, I'm the Servant of Death. Come on kid, get real."

"So I won't die?"

"Ah well, it would be better for me if you did. But don't remember that part when you wake up. The Shriken are deliberating your future right now. They think awful strange, so...not too sure what it will come to."

Marisa looked at her, bewildered, and then shook her head in disbelief, "You're really not that helpful."

"I hear that a lot." Death laughed. Her teeth were whiter than her skin.

—

In the morning Yaska searched the sands for Marisa's footprints. It hadn't been very windy, and Yaska eventually found the girl's tracks with ease. She followed the path as it patrolled the desert, and then eventually wandered towards the mountains. They ran right to the base, and then around the side, ending at a cave.

"You are not supposed to go into the mountains, Marisa," Yaska mumbled.

She entered the cave and looked around. She saw a warped Plainkind dart on the ground and picked it up. Something had put enough pressure on the sword to bend it. Plainkind weaponry was made of a notoriously stiff metal alloy. It was hard and could hold a surgical edge, but it remained tough. It didn't shatter like other metals of similar stiffness. Yaska shook her head and looked around the cave, her eyes adjusting to the dark. She saw many paths, and also a trail of sand leading from the entrance. She followed it, but it curiously led her to a dead end. Yaska looked at Marisa's sword and then into the tunnels of the cave. Then, she began her search.

3

"We cannot let this information return to the Plainkind people. It could ruin their civilization, or, as it has in the past, ruin both theirs and ours. That it is a Plainkind girl, Marisa, who knows of it only makes our deliberation more difficult."

The light-haired Shriken, Sikt, crossed his arms. He sat at a circular stone table. There was room for five but at the moment there were only two others, Jolanin and Ettin.

Jolanin nodded, "But what can we do? Perhaps we can swear her to secrecy and send her back."

The dark-haired man, Ettin, shook his head, "We cannot logically trust her. Not only is she a Plainkind, and therefore immature, but she is young even by the standards of the Plainkind people. Can we truly believe someone who is so comparatively infantile could keep such a thing secret?"

"Further," Sikt added, "you do not know the girl, or how trustworthy she may be despite what Ettin has said. You have spoken for mere minutes."

"Fair. We cannot consider her trustworthy," Jolanin said. She searched for an alternative. "Do we have a way of removing the memory of the Plainkind-Shriken lifecycle?"

Ettin looked at her skeptically, "If you knew which part of her mind it was stored, perhaps we could deliberately damage it, but that seems to me to be..."

"Unhelpful and unreliable," Jolanin agreed.

"And unnecessarily destructive. Barbaric even. Perhaps," Ettin continued, "the most reliable thing to do is to take her life."

"Surely we would not!" Jolanin said.

"I agree that we should not," Sikt said, "however what Ettin said of its reliability is certainly true."

Jolanin's first thought was to plea for the girl's life, but she thought better. That Sikt had not already agreed with Ettin's proposal implied that he may have another idea. She turned her eyes to Sikt's with this intent.

"... However," Sikt continued, breaking their gaze, "it would be just as reliable simply to not allow her to return home."

Jolanin said, "And imprison her here, with the Shriken?"

"Is it worse than death?" Sikt said.

"Keeping a person alive requires a lot of resources," Ettin said, "and she will not even be a full Shriken for possibly a century. That the girl will be a burden to someone for decades. I am unsure if a Plainkind is developed enough to contribute most Shriken occupations."

Jolanin figured that, as the one who found the girl, she would likely have to volunteer to care for Marisa, but she did not say anything. For now, she waited.

After a silence, Sikt said, "I will bring the issue and what we have discussed to the other two. The five of us will meet again in one day."

—

In the morning of the next day, Yaska and Jan left the Plainkind village together. Yaska headed north to continue her search for Marisa, and Jan headed east to cover Yaska and Marisa's hunting duties. He was getting old, but he would still be able to hunt two people's worth for a few days, Yaska knew.

—

Marisa lay on the bed of the room. She was accustomed to sleeping on skins covering the sandy desert ground. This bed was a grand improvement. She thought about her dream, of meeting Death. Was that an omen, then, that she was going to die? Even in the dream, Death herself hadn't been sure.

Jolanin announced herself then entered. Marisa didn't like the expression of frustration that the Shriken wore.

"What is it?" Marisa stood, "don't tell me my dream was right! I'm going to be killed after all, aren't I!"

Jolanin, no longer concerned with how to approach the topic, said, "We have, as of now, not yet decided. Either it will either be just as you said, or you will be confined from returning to the Plainkind and remain here. As one of us, in a certain sense. We are unsure as to how you would be able to contribute."

"So what, I'll never be able to go home? And I'll be stuck here as some sort of pet or something?"

"Perhaps you have a better solution?"

"I—I just won't tell anyone what happened!"

"The Shriken do not trust you."

"I..." Marisa fell back onto the bed and hung her face in her hands. Then, suddenly, she looked up, "So you haven't even decided!"

"No," Jolanin said, a little confused, "the entire council will be meeting later today."

"Neither Death nor you have any idea what's going to happen to me," she said, frustrated, "What's the big deal with the life cycle anyway?"

Jolanin didn't know what to make of her mention of the Servant of Death, but she did know how to answer the question about the cycle. She brought the stone chair from the desk closer to the bed and sat. "I will explain to you why the life cycle of the Plainkind to Shriken is so important. There was a time over three millennia ago when the Shriken were quite advanced. More advanced than the Solune in the east, or the Djeb in the west. I could go into detail of the mythological reasons why, but I think it is enough to say that we were enabled in part by the Servant of Birth. Then his favour left us and the civilization fell, like a table whose fourth leg suddenly breaks or...vanishes.

"During that time, we had a two tiered society. The Plainkind were an integrated part of the Shriken civilization. Without the Servant of Birth, the civilization became too complex to maintain and it collapsed. The Shriken of the time sought to preserve what was left. We archived the knowledge here in the mountains."

"Great," Marisa said, "but seriously, what does this have to do with anything?"

"The Plainkind do not know, but at the age of one-hundred-and-twenty, they begin to change into a Shriken, to become a pre-Shriken. Their skin grows many layers and they are trapped in their bodies, locked in primal mental state as their rational mind recedes inwards. They become fearsome, and wild on the outside, but deep within the psyche, thoughts lock into place. Reason hardens, and through meditation...we master mathematic and physical principals. After years in this state, the Shriken hatches, stronger, and winged; and also with this new genius, ready to join our civilization. Then, we live to three-hundred and promptly die."

"Wait," Marisa stood up, "the Plainkind can live that long? I thought ninety was old, that's a whole thirty years more! And then after, what, you get almost two more lifespans?"

"And now comes the reason it is kept a secret. There have been a few times that Plainkind people have learned of their potential for an extended mortality. Generally what happens is that they become selfish, and single-mindedly focus on keeping themselves alive. You are too young. They orient their lives towards becoming Shriken, even at the expense of the people around them. They become tyrannical in order to amass resources in order to sustain themselves.

"Shriken records state that once, an entire village collaborated to this end. They gave up having offspring in order to have fewer mouths to feed; less resources to gather. An entire generation hit the transitory period in a short time frame. Then, they became pre-Shriken, and...oh youth, you do not know. This form can last years. They roamed the deserts wildly terrorizing other villages, consuming prey, and in many cases killing each other. We had to come down and protect the Plainkind by driving them into the treacherous sands of the west.

"The long-term effects of that were more subtle but quite nearly as disruptive. For us, a large amount of these self-minded Shriken entered our civilization. For the Plainkind, an entire village exited the ecosystem and economy of the desert. You may have heard stories of Village #5, in the north west?"

Marisa nodded. It was a myth, most questioned if it ever existed at all. They were known as the ore suppliers. Apparently they had mastered hot forging, and supplied the best hunting and medical tools to the other four villages. It was a lost city, a land of bounty and natural treasure. Now, most of the ore was mined by her village, and Village #4. She shook her head. "So it was real..."

"Centuries ago. I am honestly surprised that it survived in your orature for so long. It is for reasons such as these that the Plainkind cannot know that they might become Shriken. The lifecycle must remain a secret from them."

Marisa stared, wide-eyed. "We are too selfish..."

"...Only because it takes us longer to mature than most of our neighbours."

The room was silent for a long period of time as the girl's mind delved into thought.

"So," she began, "normally the Plainkind that become Shriken do it accidentally, by living long enough."

"When they begin to change, they naturally urge to wander into the desert away from people to 'die.' Generally one of us will notice and move them to the west where their wild nature is of less consequence."

"And what, with all this knowledge that you saved from back when you were all advanced, have the Shriken been, I don't know, trying to rebuild the old system? So then you won't have to worry about all these secrets?"

Jolanin was taken aback, "Rebuild the ancient civilization? Without Birth?"

Marisa shrugged, "You said that the Servant of Birth was only one of the, uh, four legs, right? If you could build most of it on your own, why can't you figure out what Birth contributed and just work towards that yourself?"

"It is an interesting idea, but I do not believe it possible," Jolanin stood, "I have to meet with the rest of the council. When I return, you will know what will become of you."

Marisa watched Jolanin exit the room. She lay back on the bed and tried to sleep. She hoped that if she napped she might see the Servant of Death again. Anything was better than sitting around worrying.

Outside, Jolanin headed back towards the meeting room. She considered Marisa's proposition, but figured it impossible. Instead, she focused her mind on the decision that was coming.

—

Yaska had searched both the mountain in which she found Marisa's sword, and the foot of the mountain to its right. She was now sitting at the mouth of the cave where she started, finishing a lunch. She stood and turned her eyes to the mountain on the left. It was the last place she could think to look, unless some creature had simply consumed Marisa whole. As she walked, Yaska considered this. She was probably capable of slaying all the beasts in the desert if she needed to, but if Marisa had been eaten, doing so wouldn't change much.

She headed toward the mountain.

—

Marisa awoke to Jolanin's voice, and then the sound of the stone door opening. She had successfully fallen asleep, but had dreamt nothing. She sat up, got out of bed, and then looked at Jolanin. The Shriken's face was expressionless.

"There was an external issue, thus the council felt itself forced to this decision. You are to be killed."

4

Marisa rubbed her eyes, "What?"

The women looked at each other until Marisa's mind registered what had been said.

"No! I have to... I have to return to my village! I only left to hunt, I shouldn't be here. Just let me leave." She groped for anything, "I, I escaped, didn't I? Yeah, just let me go, and tell them all that I escaped."

Jolanin was disheartened, "It is a good idea, but it cannot be done."

"Why! Why do they suddenly want to kill me? Before I at least had the option of being a pet."

"I will explain. It appears that there is a young, grey haired Plainkind woman looking for you. As you know, we have many reasons why we do not want others searching the mountain. The conclusion the Shriken have taken to is...we will plant your dead body near some cave. We will give her reason to end her search. I am to execute you."

Marisa knew that the woman must be Yaska, but she wasn'0t comforted by the deduction.

"What if...what if you and I, we pretend I'm dead. Then you can plant me, and Yaska will find me not dead, but alive!"

Jolanin was going to object, that it would be impossible to pass a living body as a dead one to a Shriken, but before she could say anything, a third voice spoke.

"You really think that would work?"

Jolanin's eyes shot about the room. Marisa thought she recognized the voice.

Death stepped into the room from between the desk's shadow and the lamplight. She bared her teeth in a grin. Her face was pale blue, and sickly in its colourlessness.

"How did you get in here?" Jolanin asked.

"You know how. What, don't you Shriken have some knowledge of things like this?"

Jolanin's eyes narrowed, "So, then, you are the Servant of Death. You do not look as I was led to believe."

"What, did you think I'd be dead too? Quite an ineffective state to have to work in, don't you think?" She grinned again.

Marisa's mind raced through her situation. Had Death come to kill her? No, Death isn't generally the cause of death, just the beneficiary. Was she here because of the execution then? Why would she bother? Was it because of the dream? Was she really even there? The questions swirled in her mind until she blurted out, "Do you finally know if I'm going to die?"

Death stopped berating the Shriken and turned to Marisa, frowning. "I already told you that I don't know. Not enough has changed. I can read minds, what's let out anyway, but the Shriken think in math...I really only know binary. Living? Or dead.... Anyway, are both of you going to be this foolish the entire time I'm here?" The Servant of Death shook her head and shrugged. She wasn't wearing her overcoat this time and her shoulders peeked out from beneath her raven hair. "I have other things to do, you know. Well...no I don't. This world figures out death pretty well on its own."

Marisa stood up indignantly. "If you don't know whether I'm going to die why show up in the first place? Why are you even here?"

Death sighed, "Could you at least show some reverence? I am an immortal Servant after all. Or at least fear? I happen to be a somewhat arbitrary killer you know. That's how I pass the time most days." She eyed the room, then continued, "As one you know, I've been paying attention to this situation. I find it interesting. I'm here to propose a trade."

Marisa stared at her, "A–A trade? What could I, here, possibly have to trade you?"

"Just you, who is to be executed regardless, being a part of the trade is enough for me. Things don't tend to go to well if I tell them too much ahead of time anyway."

"Unacceptable," Jolanin said, "on the Plainkind's behalf, I must insist that your terms make for horrid negotiation."

"Well, that's not for you to decide anyway. Unless you want to take matters into your own hands and kill the girl now," she bared her teeth, "at least, Marisa, let me tell you your end of the trade."

"Fine. So far it seems you're the person who least wants to kill me."

"That is not true!" Jolanin said, "I just think it is best to understand first what—"

Death interrupted her, "Yeah, well, here's your half anyway. In return for your part Marisa, you, well most of you, will be able to return to your village. And you, Shriken...Jolanin, will have your body for the council. Hell, I'll even take the memories out."

Marisa looked at Death in amazement. Jolanin looked with scepticism.

Death smiled, "I'll leave you alone for a minute to decide." Before waiting for a reply, the Servant of Death covered herself in the desk's shadow and was gone.

Marisa shuddered.

Jolanin said, "I do not think it wise to make a trade with Death."

"It's too good to be true," Marisa said, "but the only other option is to die, so..."

"I am certain there is some sort of trick behind Death's paradoxical offers. But, to choose her offer over your execution is logical. Not that I would do it."

"What would you do?"

"I would fight my way either to freedom or to death."

Marisa was silent.

"Be wary that, more likely than not, something terribly unusual is bound to be done to you should you take Death's offer." Jolanin unsheathed the sword she had brought for the execution, just in case.

At this point, Death returned.

"So," she said, "have you decided?"

Marisa said, "Yes. I will take your offer."

"Wonderful! I haven't gotten a chance to do this in a while."

She approached Marisa and stuck her finger, as if she were a ghost, through Marisa's chest, then removed it. Adrenaline rushed to Marisa's heart, and with each pump seethed into her blood. Her anxiety levels, as a result, spiked. Her hair turned bright white, even her body hair, giving her whole body a soft glow.

"Ah! No! What's happening?" Marisa shouted.

The Servant looked at her with dead eyes, but said nothing. Marisa's eyes widened, then her body began to shimmer. The girl's image was becoming distorted, as if through a desert haze. She dropped to her knees and her outline doubled, and then, as if crawling from the girl's back, a second image split apart from her.

Marisa turned to face the second being, and looked into a face nearly identical to her own. Except for the black in her eyes where the whites should have been and the fact that, while Marisa's wore an expression of irrational anxiety and her hair glowed white, the double's expression was one filled with irrational rage. It emerged entirely from Marisa, kneeling behind her, and then it took the girl in a stranglehold.

"What is the meaning of this?" Jolanin said.

"Well, I'm actually not entirely sure why this keeps happening. I have a few guesses myself. Usually—actually no, every time, I just let things play out. More for me! Though, sometimes I don't watch. It can get pretty..."

Jolanin stopped listening and went to Marisa, whose girl's face had turned red, and tentatively thrust her sword towards the double.

The double let go of Marisa after being stabbed superficially, her arm shooting towards the Shriken's hand. Taking advantage of Jolanin's surprise, she wrenched the weapon away and swung it downward, impaling Marisa with it. Jolanin took her sword back and kicked the duplicate, launching her into the wall. She then rushed to Marisa and rolled her over.

For Marisa, the world had become slow. Her hair went back to its natural sandy-blonde. Her mind turned. She thought of what would have happened if she hadn't come the cave. She thought further back to her times hunting, and living in the village, of her mother, and other things.

"Jolanin, thanks for trying..." she said. She felt a deep affection for this woman. Where had it come from? It didn't matter.

Death did something in the corner as she watched the girl die, still talking of the many other times she had caused this to happen.

Jolanin watched her. The execution sword had fulfilled its task perfectly, and had ripped a clean hole through the girl's chest. The Shriken took her sword and thrust it with uncanny speed through the girl's neck, slicing surgically though both spinal columns. Marisa died instantly from the execution.

"And then I thought, perhaps everyone is angry when they're born. Infants tend to be awfully loud. I asked the Servant of Birth about it, and he said that probably wasn't it. Oh, I got her memories by the way, see?" Death held absolutely nothing between her two hands.

"Have not you any empathy?" Jolanin asked.

Death shrugged. Indifferent. "Would you believe me if I said I see this all the time?"

Jolanin looked to the Marisa that was alive. She had calmed down.

She asked Death, "What is this person? Why did she kill Marisa?"

"Well, I've kind of been telling you my theories this whole time...? Anyway, I call it a double. She's mostly the same as the original, but there are some differences, usually a couple of inverted inclinations. My best guess as to why the double immediately wants kill the original is that the double is mostly a creation of mine. So their first instinct would be related to me, Servant of Death. And what I do is...well." She shrugged, as a natural philosopher might after watching a fox kill another over food.

Jolanin looked at the girl. It was true that there were differences, at least physically. Her eyes were, in a sense, inverted. The whites were black, and the irises white. She had no visible pupil.

"The little differences I've seen, other than the eyes, were personality, interests, things like that. Oh, and she does have pupils, but they reflect a lot of white, like a deer, you know? They're there, just hard to see. The double may also take a name that's similar to the original, but slightly modified. Look. Hey!" Death turned to the newly created girl. "What are you called?"

The double looked up from ground, "Mariça."

"Now." She turned back to Jolanin, and threw the ball of nothing she held at the girl. "Watch this. What can you tell me about the Shriken life cycle?"

Mariça's expression faltered, "Uh, I guess they have children? Who grow up to...have more, and so on?"

"She doesn't remember?" Jolanin said.

"Eh, more like she never knew," Death said, "as promised." She looked again to Mariça and said, "It'll be nice to see what comes of you."

Then, she returned to the lamplight and covered herself in its shadow.

Mariça and Jolanin were left staring at each other. The Shriken looked at the body of Marisa, and then at Mariça.

"Well, I guess both our problems have been solved. And what has happened was as I had said, terribly unusual. All that is left is to take the body to the council, and find a way to get you out."

"Okay, but," Mariça said, "where am I?"

5

Jolanin had explained very basically to Mariça that she had been captured because she had entered too deep into Shriken territory. Then she'd left Mariça alone in order to take the dead body to the council. Mariça spent her alone time sitting in the room and trying to figure in her mind what was going on. Memories began to come to her, as if from outside her head. As if from someone else's head, some long lost sibling that existed only in a brief dream.

Everything that had happened to Marisa before the incident with Death began to leak into her own brief experiences. Mariça remembered what it had felt like to be Marisa, right up until then end. What a sinister memory for Death to leave. Everything returned, despite what the Servant of Death had said. She remembered all about the life cycle. Something moved in the corner, and she heard a woman's laughter. Mariça tried to remember exactly how she got here. She had the sudden urge to sneeze, but instead, an unusual sensation came over her.

"I entered a cave. I saw a Shriken. She was nice to me, but kept me here while they figured out what to do with me. They wanted to kill me because...because."

"And, as they swim near your head, I just cut here and here, and now you'll never find out. I killed some of your memories, dear! Well, don't worry too much. You're dead, but you'll be mostly fine. I think. I'm interested in seeing how the other woman reacts, your friend." The voice came from somewhere near her head, and then moved closer to the desk with the lamp. Shortly after the voice finished talking, the flickering flame went out, leaving Mariça in darkness.

The details of why she was here, and why the Shriken wanted her dead, were gone. She just had them, but it was like she had wakened from a vivid dream only to forget it all. She did remember dying though, and then with a sickening lurch, she realized that the body Jolanin had taken away was her own. She shook her head, got dizzy, and decided to lie down. She curled up into a foetal position, and stared at the dark nothing beside the bed.

When Jolanin finally returned, Mariça had mostly figured out her situation through her the cold panic, except for the bits that Death had cut away and evaporated.

Jolanin said, "The body has been planted, and we have also seen your friend searching near it. There is someone monitoring the situation to make sure that she finds the body and gives up her search."

"Okay. What about me?"

"No one knows about your existence, and it would be best for you if it remained that way. I will escort you out in secret, but it will be after your friend finds the body and the scout leaves."

"But won't that mean Yaska will think I'm dead?"

"This is the only way to keep the Shriken from knowing about you. It will be unfortunate for her, but in a very literal sense you are dead."

Mariça shook her head. "I am...not."

—

Yaska sat near the Shriken's mountain, eating strips of dried meat dinosaur. She had searched for two days straight, not even returning to the village, and had found nothing besides Marisa's bent sword. She stood and returned to her task. It wasn't long after that she found a set of tracks in the sand. She was immediately suspicious. The tracks should have blown away overnight, so they must be recent. Yaska checked her feet against them and confirmed that the tracks were not her own. She then followed them.

She was led into another cave, and in it she found the body of Marisa. Yaska was gripped by dread. She put her hand in her hair. Her breathing became shallow. A tear ran from her eye.

But then she took a breath. She would postpone her emotion until the burial. Right now it was more important to take Marisa, and the story of what had happened, back to the village. Yaska knelt down by the corpse. She thought it was strange that the body was so cold. It seemed like it had been dead for more than a day. Were the tracks Marisa's, or someone else's? She lifted the body. Its blood was dry, and none of it had pooled on the ground. Yaska's scepticism heightened. As respectfully as such an act allowed, she tested the body's its feet against the footprints outside. She hosted the body over her shoulder. They were not hers. She would have to return later.

—

Mariça followed Jolanin through the Shriken temple. She was wearing a cloak to hide her face in case they were seen. They moved through the stone halls that cut cleanly through the mountains. Everything was empty for the most part. Jolanin said that they were passing through a residential area, and that everyone had been gone since morning.

"If we do see someone, act as though you belong. Keep your eyes down. We do not need questions about them."

Mariça nodded and they continued for a few more minutes, until they did encounter another Shriken. It was a man holding a box. He stopped when he saw them.

"Oh! Jolanin, I was, ah, just getting something from home. Why are you here?"

Mariça, keeping her had down, looked at the man's feet. She couldn't see anything else.

Jolanin replied, "I am showing someone where to go."

Before the man could ask anything else, Jolanin continued walking. Mariça kept her head down, and followed the other woman's feet. Eventually they stopped, and Mariça looked up. There was an inconspicuous looking wall at the end of the hall. The only thing unusual about it was how natural it looked in contrast with the planed surfaces of the halls up to this point.

Jolanin said, "We are at the exit."

"Thanks, for all you've done for me."

Jolanin smiled, "You are welcome. Remember though, that had there not been interference, I would have had to execute you."

Mariça frowned, "Would you have?"

For a moment Jolanin paused, reflecting. She said, "I might have tried your method of faking your death. And, if it had failed, I may well have chosen to fight our way out. Although, I am unsure as to where that would have left us."

Mariça laughed.

"Well," Jolanin continued, "we might meet again if you—" she stopped herself.

"If I what? See you when you're outside the mountain?"

Jolanin nodded, "Perhaps I will see you outside the mountains. You might watch the skies for me, I suppose." Jolanin grabbed at a couple of jagged edges in the wall and pulled the whole section upwards, revealing the outside.

"Your friend is in that direction," she pointed, "you may want to find her before she leaves or becomes too distressed."

"Thanks." Mariça gave her gratitude and then left, following the edge of the mountain where Jolanin had pointed.

It wasn't long before the Plainkind girl saw someone, a stout female figure with a person over one shoulder, walking away from the mountain. Mariça stopped. Seeing her own body in person—it was uncanny. She realized that she wasn't sure how to approach her old friend. Marisa's friend. What would happen when she saw her?

As Mariça pondered this, Yaska's attentive eyes fixed on her and adjusted. She stopped walking and stared. Unsure what Yaska would do, Mariça raised her arm in greeting. She guessed that Yaska would approach, but that she might also assault her, or even ignore her. It was hard to tell what someone would to when faced with an apparent impossibility.

It seemed Yaska decided to approach in a leisurely pace. She carefully laid the corpse on the sand. She seemed to study it before looking again in Mariça's direction. Then, she unclasped the sword from her back and approached slowly.

Mariça was unarmed. She didn't want to die again, and she wasn't sure what she would do if things went poorly. She decided to believe in Marisa's friend...or was she her friend?

Slowly, the two women met. They looked at each other. Yaska said nothing, and they stood there for a long time. Mariça began to think that she might leave. Was she waiting? Did she want to take a reactive stance? Mariça wasn't sure. She decided to speak first.

"Yaska."

Yaska waited for more. When she saw that there wasn't going to be any more, she said, "How do you know my name?"

"I, ah..."

"She," Yaska pointed, "knew my name. How do you?"

"I, I took—I mean, I have most of her memories."

"Fine." That seemed to be enough for her in that respect. She then asked, "Who are you?"

"I'm Mariça."

Yaska frowned, "Marisa?"

"No, Mariça."

"Mariça."

"Yes."

Yaska paused. She considered Mariça, and she considered Marisa. "You are slightly different in name, and in face. And your hair is lighter. It is an unnatural pink. Are you aware?"

Mariça took a lock of her hair from the side of her head, and brought it to her eyes. "Oh."

"Fine," Yaska said again, "well, come. The village has been worried about—" she paused, "worried about most of you."

Yaska picked up Marisa's corpse and she and Mariça headed back to the village. As they walked, they spoke to each other. Mariça did her best to recount to Yaska what had happened. It was a good conversation for both of them, but they each got an unnerving feeling.

When the two had returned to the village, they agreed to be honest about the strange situation, and Marisa was buried. Mariça's mother remained silent and stone faced during the burial. Afterwards, she got to know Mariça well enough to recognise her, and accepted her as a responsibility. Things started this way, and as the days passed, they got better. The village returned to normal, except for one thing.

—

Mariça threw her sword, and it stuck in the back leg of the dinosaur. Now that it was slowed, she chased the creature down and took her sword out and in the same motion, swung around, cutting into the beast's neck.

What next? She thought back to Marisa's experiences, and then she the sword out and cut again, over and over until the head disconnected. She took the leather bag she had brought and put it around the stump to save the blood. Then, she buried the head as an offering, and prayed.

It was shortly after midday when she returned to the village. Yaska came a little after.

"You are a lot better at hunting," she said.

Mariça nodded, "From what I can remember, I was always this good just...distracted."

"Well," Yaska said, "I can help Jan open these. You have time to go out exploring, if you wish."

"Yeah, I guess I do, but...maybe some other time."

"Do you not have the desire to?" Yaska looked into the distance. "I wonder how much has changed."

Mariça shrugged, "I can remember the feeling of wanting to, but I haven't properly felt it since we returned." She looked at Yaska with her inverted eyes.

"Yes...perhaps that is it. In this, I have changed."

The Young Spectator

She peered around the doorway, through the entrance. The room was full, as it usually was at this time. Would she learn about those things during her schooling? Possibly, but it would be in later years. She came often and didn't think anyone noticed her when she sneaked in, but there was one who always did. The oration had started a few minutes ago, so the room's attention was fixed at the front. Charllotte crept in. Everyone's focus was at the front. She crouched as she moved, but one person saw her. He always saw her obliviously creep in and sit on the floor behind the rear barriers. Today, the man decided to nudge his partner, a woman even older than him, and point her out. The woman saw and stifled a gasp.

The courtroom was made almost entirely of metal, an unfortunate material. The walls were covered with cloth drapings and the floor with a grand carpet, leaving the place feeling almost like a castle with tapestries and rugs. Charllotte didn't know the alloys. She knew quite a lot for her age, that is what people told her, but of metals, she had learned very little. She crawled behind the benches. There was only one more gap to cross and she would be at her hiding spot. Anyone not requested to attend was allowed in, and worse, only those with age of majority identification papers could spectate. She had to sneak in like this.

"Ah-ha! I knew you were trying to avoid section sixteen!"

Someone shouted, startling her, and freezing her in place for a moment. The call echoed across the walls and ceiling. (He whispered, explaining that this girl came to trials quite frequently. She asked him why, but interrupted by one of the speakers.) The call moved to her end of the room with noticeable a degree of control. Charllotte caught herself, and glanced down the second gap between the benches. She could see the man who had called out, pale and confident, on the other side of the room. He continued speaking as he had before. His yell had been made on purpose, that man must have practiced in order to make such an effect. Charlotte wished she had come earlier.

Then Charllotte saw eyes on her, beyond the orator. She gasped—not just one, but two judges had seen her. She scurried forward out of sight. Two judges had noticed her! She sat hidden in the corner. She breathed hard through her mouth, as quietly as she could. Usually, she listened and studied what was happening by ear and then escape before everything ended. She had been doing this for so long and getting away unseen, but now someone had noticed her. And it was a judge! Two judges!

She was hidden in the corner, in a little nook created by the wall on two sides, and the barrier and its open door on the other. She breathed hard, but through her mouth, as quietly as she could. Surprisingly, after the case was decided and the courtroom emptied, no one bothered to look over the barrier to where she was hiding. At least, she didn't think so. Usually, Charllotte listened and studied by ear what happened in the court. Then, would leave before everything ended, but today she was shaken. Would she ever be able to sneak in again? Would she be caught? What would the judges do? Her brain swirled, and just as the thought leaving—leaving immediately and running—just as the idea occurred to her, the steel whistle blew and ended the session.

She waited, and then looked up to check if everyone had left. She didn't want to be surprised again. As the footsteps faded, Charllotte caught her breath, and readied herself to make a dash out through the door. She stood up and stopped.

"There she is," said the male judge.

Her body tensed again. He had waited for her! Both judges had. "Ah!" Her call was short and loud. She tried to stifle it, but it echoed across the iron ceiling.

"Ah!"

Her call was short, but loud. She tried to stifle it, but it reverberated across the courtroom.

"This isn't the time for silliness!"

It was the second judge, the woman. She was taller than Charllotte would have expected of a woman that old. She was dark and also very wrinkled, with eyes Charllotte felt could read her mind through her face.

"It wasn't too bad a shout, I don't think." The other judge, the old man, mumbled. He mumbled, but unusually loud. And he was nodding continuously, but very slightly, giving his head an odd agreeable bob. "Maybe with some practice she could be rhetorician. Just need to work on your self-control a bit." At this, he laughed, but without smiling. It was a mirthful laugh, but it confused her more than anything else.

"Umm," Charllotte started to turn towards the door. Both of the judges were in the benches, and they were both elderly. She could quite likely run and lose them quite easily.

"Stop there, maid." The woman spoke sharply, but her eyes were even worse.

"You can't call her maid," the man mumbled noisily, "this generation doesn't even know what that means, do you?" He laughed plainfacedly and wiped his face. He had light skin that seemed to have been hardened by the sun, as if he had been slowly cooking all his life.

Charllotte frantically tried to find in her head a sentence, even a single word to say in reply. Instead, to her tense relief, the woman interrupted her.

"Why are you here?"

Charllotte gave up trying to form arguments or excuses. She gave up and just spoke.

"I came here to learn!"

"Learn courts?" Said the man.

"How old are you, five?" Asked the woman.

"No no, she must be eleven or twelve. Come on Shushann, don't you have grandchildren?" He laughed again.

"Five, eleven, same thing under these circumstances. A child. So you're breaking how many rules?" Shushann asked.

"Two," Charllotte said.

"At least that."

"And?" The man said, to Charllotte's surprise. "What are we going to do about it? I vote nothing. Come now, you are the only other judge here, what is your vote?"

"She must be punished."

Charllotte stepped back.

The man laughed. "What punishment then!"

"I—"

"I vote nothing," the man said.

The Shushann frowned. "You mustn't come here anymore. Not until you reach adulthood."

Banned? She was banned! She had been exiled from the courthouse! Why? She had come here only to learn on the topic which fascinated her most. She wasn't breaking any rules; she wasn't breaking any rules that made sense to her anyway. But she would never be allowed to return here. Never again...

Charllotte began to cry.

Shushann took a step back in disbelief. "I am not—Fordrick, you have grandchildren, do what must be done!"

What must be done? Charllotte began to cry out louder. It echoed across the ceiling and across to the other end of the room and back again, but with the added sharpness of the steel walls. Fordrick closed the door.

"Come now, you have to save that crying talent for when you are trying to warp the reason of judges in your next trial, child." He chuckled, but this time he actually put in the effort to smile. And the wrinkles in his face did funny things when he smiled. They bunched up around his forehead and his mouth, but his cheeks puffed up and become smooth and shiny. Charllotte laughed.

"Tell me, how old are you?"

She wiped her eyes and took a breath. She was eleven. She could take control of her emotions at least somewhat, being this old, and so she decided to show them. She said, "I am eleven."

"Well, there you go Shushann."

"What."

"She's eleven."

"So?"

"So," he turned back to the girl, "tell me, young, err..."

He trailed off, and Charllotte said, "Err? No, my name isn't err."

"Err, no it isn't. It is..."

He trailed off again, this time it looked like he was trailing off into a nap as well. (He wasn't though, he was just trying to be silly to keep the girl's spirits up.) Shushann opened the door again.

"I am Charllotte."

"That's an awfully long name! Tell me, when is your birth date?"

"Birth date? Why, it is—" her eyes lit up. Fordrick straightened up and smiled. Shushann watched in amazement as she read the girl. Her face revealed the connections being made within. The girl had figured it out, and Fordrick knew...and she didn't even know.

"My birthday is in two months!"

"And, of course, you wouldn't want to continue breaking the law now would you?" Fordrick asked.

"No, of course not. But!"

"But what?"

"Stop," Shushann said. "One moment. What are you two talking about? I can read a face, but I cannot read your minds."

"Why, when she's twelve, is she not legally an adult?" Fordrick smiled.

"But..." Charllotte mumbled.

"Yes," Shushann added, "but who says she can attend trials that she is not required to?"

"Oh." Fordrick stopped. Then, he began to smile slightly.

Charllotte nodded and frowned. Then she saw Shushann's expression.

"Why, at thirteen, are you not considered old enough?" Fordrick smiled.

"Thirteen is not the age of majority," Shushann added. Then, her eyes widened. "Oh, I see, you intend to give her a student observer's pass, do you?"

"Ah!" Charllotte's mouth opened up. "Ah!" Charllotte's mouth opened up. "I know about that! That is *'a document permitting a young person currently enrolled in any Lussa academy to observe valid and open trials.'*"

"Yes, that is the law...almost as written," said Shushann. "You don't, by any chance happen to read law books too, do you? At five years old?"

Charllotte stopped, a little confused. She looked at Fordrick, who smiled back.

She said, "No, no. I couldn't read when I was four. But I can read now, and I have, a little."

One Man's Fantasy – Sermon I

Jn th' place thov hast seen   only in uiſions dither hence
Silver cloods and litle   dreams that thither deep inſide
The skool, from inſide you meditate yovr way to playces
Higher than the cloods   a place a freedom far from hær
You can diue and dance   act with no fær

A land yov'u conjured in your mind   a place in a falſe light?
Still you moue your palmes   conſtruct a kingdom glory pouer might
To exercise a protestacioun   no more warres you'll have to fight
Yet as you dub courtieres   with honour, someone tilets a head
She aſks you how you got here,   From what land were you led, king?

Somehow she urges you to honeſty   meditation, is what yov saye
Cartesian? No no, you saye   What then? Eclectic, you saye.
She lovghes at your ansvver   it is fooljsh to her, and yet,   she says,
Here you are. What will you   do to this land you have?
She shaykes her hed,   disappointment in face.

She canst if you heard   the words she hadde,
Wenen wisly that it be nat so   passe over your mind & land.   she says,
Maybe next time,   she says, musically, as a muse ought,
Then flovrishing her long   golden locks, she ties her hair,
Rhye, Prince of the Solune,   leaving the cerebral game unfovght.

Decades, scores, paſs by   and in your diminiſhed age,   she returns.
Shocked, aſking her why   she hasn't aged a moment, she turns,
Pouren down on you now   arced over a cane,   she says,
Sire, why, she says,   neither have you.
Why are you still here,   after so long?

This is a place of concept, she says, a place for the
Mind to open and see   I thought you'd have known better, and
Set your own thoughts free,   but instead you kept to the phantasy.
In this place, you will never   be free (so be free!)

Trapped in here forever   a form of madness,   she says,
She waxes unencumbered   have you ever wondered,   she says,
Have you never ever wondered   what this place is?   she says,

This is the vvorld of my   own command,   you saye,
It heeds my beck and call   I am in controll here, royalty   & all
This is a higher world of thought, open only to a few,   she says,

A pity that you've ruined it   since you had met me too.
No one disobeys here   because here there is nobody else;
No consciousness at all   The only life in here,   apart from you, is me.

You know I thought I had created here,   but really it seems I'd not.
This is a shared headspace   t'was first a legend where Plato thought
There was a world of forms   that I took a step further I ought
You come here in your thoughts alone,   to stay here, mind is rife.
And your thoughts are...wrong   so if you want to live your life,   then
Yovr next steps shovld be obuious   though they may cauſe you strife.

And all this time you knew that   if you heard the worlds I've said,
You'd haue to leaue this playce   and re-turn to yovr conscious life.

Starman

Jan was telling a story about the storm festival. Yaska rubbed her fingers through the sand. It did not rain a lot in the desert, but every second year at the same time, there was a rainstorm. This was the marker, the Plainkind new year. Even though she had been away from her community for ages, Yaska had heard his story many times and had gotten bored of it. She decided to leave the fireside story, walk out of the village, and go look at the stars. Time, it was fascinating. Everywhere else, they used the stars, since they didn't have such storms. One Plainkind year, Yaska had found, was equal to around two astral years.

"Where are you going?" It was her friend Mariça, the most unusual looking of the tribe.**

"West. I am going to look at the stars."

"Okay."

Yaska walked until she couldn't hear the buzz of the gathering. She found a spot next to a shrub and lay down, resting her hands behind her head. It wasn't always easy to see the stars when she travelled because the heat in the atmosphere often distorted anything too high. In her homelands, however, there was less humidity. Here she could see. Even on this clear night, the stars shimmered and danced in the skies. Yaska gazed thoughtfully. She knew she was only seeing a fraction of them. She gazed at the shining dots above her, tracking them with her eyes until she saw one that was shifting in an irregular pattern. She blinked. It wasn't shimmering, or moving in hazy circles. It was shuddering, and getting brighter. Yaska watched it, and realized that it was brightening because it was growing. She sat up, and then, keeping her eye on the star, she stood. She rubbed her eyes, and when she opened them again, the light was the size of her fist.

"What?"

A fiery mass plummeted down from the heavens. Yaska watched as it smashed into the ground, twenty steps in front of her. She was quite astonished. Yaska, fearless, approached the landing area. As the smoke dissipated, she could see a bright mass of whites and yellows shifting around just above the ground. She watched as the ball of light took shape. It morphed vertically, splitting at the bottom and the sides. She watched it compress into the definite shape of a person.

"...Hello?"

The form's brightness faded slowly, until all that remained was a soft glow over its tanned skin. The face remained featureless.

Yaska waved her hand in front of where the face should have been. She thought that perhaps that would spark the next part of the creature's transformation, that maybe it had gotten stuck in the process of becoming something; someone. Yaska put her hands on her hips, staring at it. After a while of nothing happening, she took a step back.

The creature tentatively stepped forward.

"Aha!" Yaska took another step backwards, and the creature again followed. "So you can do something!"

She turned and started walking back to the village, checking over her shoulder to make sure that the creature was following. As she neared the makeshift stone huts of her village, she heard muttering.

Then, a voice rang out, "I will go, because I am the eldest. If anything happens to me, it is a much smaller loss than if we lose Jan, who is our hunter."

Yaska entered and approached the group; huddled together and worried. It was Mariça's part-mother who had volunteered herself. Jan noticed her first.

He said, "What is that following you?!"

Yaska stopped. The creature stopped. Yaska realized she had no idea what she had just led into her village. She assumed it wasn't dangerous because thus far it had been so benign, but she couldn't be sure. Still, she wasn't too worried. If it was dangerous, she would deal with it.

She turned and said, "—Oh, you are finally getting yourself a face, I see."

The face of the creature pushed itself out of the front of its head, much to the surprise of the villagers.

Jan ran up to Yaska and whispered, "Is this normal?"

Yaska nodded stating, "It started as a ball of light."

"Hey!" Jan shouted so that the group could hear, "It...it has a mouth now!"

Yaska and Jan looked up. Yaska approached the creature.

"Can you speak?"

The creature opened its mouth and gave a shriek. Jan stepped back. Yaska stepped forward, readying herself, just in case.

Mariça's mother walked to Jan and said, "that's an infant's screech. If it just got its mouth and tongue and pipes, it likely doesn't know how to use them."

Mariça said, "They look like...my lips." She took its head in his hands. "And look, ears too. I think they might be..."

"They're yours, Jan. Look, they're large." Yaska looked back and forth between her friend and the creature. "Yes..."

After tapping it a few times in different places, Mariça declared the creature harmless. Yaska said that, since it had figured out how to grow a face through observation, it would likely learn how to speak the same way. So, the village returned to the fire and Jan began another story.

And the creature listened.

—

"What? Come on, we're trying to help you!"

"I...do not have the words. I just wish to return...I need food, but not your food."

Yaska nodded, "That makes sense, you want to go home. I guess that the word for his food probably is not in Plainkind vocabulary."

"Vocabulary?" Jan asked.

Yaska said, "Vocabulary is...it is all the words you have to choose from when you speak. I learned the term from my travels. From Chloe."

"Oh yes, Chloe Rhye, the outsider. She knows quite a bit."

"Yes she does," Yaska agreed, "Chloe knows about history, and science, and...oh Jan!"

"What?" Jan asked. The Starman, too, looked at her.

"We could ask Chloe to help!"

"Oh, great idea!"

"I will write her a letter when we return. We can send it by bird."

—

Yaska, Jan, the Starman, and Chloe Rhye stood just inside the desert village, near Yaska's house.

"This is the Starman," Yaska said.

Chloe considered him. She looked at his face, and his form. The face looked similar to Mariça's, and just as cheerless. "It is growing eyes."

Yaska watched. "Your eyes. And your little upturned nose."

Chloe blushed, and said, "You know, Yaska, I doubted your letter, but...I can tell that something with this Starman is off. I need to prove it to myself."

The eyes looked around. Despite his stolen female features, he had the bone structure of Jan's ears, a broad-cheeked masculine look, but the small chin of Mariça.

"What do you mean by off?" Jan asked.

"Yaska, can you get me one of your shirts? No, not the one you're wearing right now."

Yaska shrugged. Shortly after, she returned from her small stone hut with a shirt. Chloe took the shirt and offered it to the Starman, who put it on.

Chloe asked, "Does it fit?"

"It fits exactly," he said.

Yaska's eyes widened, but Jan remained confused.

He said, "What's this about?"

Chloe addressed the Starman, "You look like a man, but you're not, are you. You just copied what's around you in order to give yourself shape. Since the person you met first was Yaska, you took on her body. We can see that he didn't have any feminine features though, he only took your frame...which is fairly masculine anyway."

Yaska flushed in response.

"I'm still lost." Jan said.

Yaska looked at the Starman. Her shirt fit the creature almost better than it fit her.

"Well, I am not lost," Yaska said, "when he landed, as Chloe said, the first person he met was me. He was just a ball of light, and then he took on my shape. Jan, do you remember when he first came to the village?"

"It had no face..."

Yaska's face became stern. She said, "It came from the sky and imitated my body. It came to the village and took on my friends' face. Then, it came to our campfire and imitated our language. What does it want, blending in with us so?" She accusingly pointed a clawed finger at the Starman, "Is getting home truly your only goal?"

Silence overcame the group. The Starman stared, searching his limited vocabulary for words with which to explain himself.

Chloe's mumbling eventually broke in, "...imitation, returning to the sky... he truly is a star, isn't he? I didn't think that the legend was true."

Jan said, "What legend?"

The Starman said, "Tell us, please."

—

Some of the villagers had gathered around Jan's fire, anticipating the story from the outsider, Chloe Rhye.

"My father told me it was long ago, I always assumed one or two thousand years. A star fell from the sky. It was unlike a dead shooting star. It was alive, and it landed on the planet. The ancient people encountered it, and came to fear it.

"The first person to find it was a great hero. The star took the shape of the hero. It was uncanny for the people, to see this false form of the hero. They accused it of being a demon, and captured it out of fear, caging it.

"The hero did not fear the star like the townspeople, instead he feared for the star. The star had done nothing wrong, but would likely be charged will all forms of frivolity, and the ancient people would decide to kill it. Standing around the star's cage, and surrounded by his people, the hero decided to take a risk to save the star.

"The hero gave a great laugh, and then pointed to the cage, 'You fools, you have captured the wrong person, for I am the star, and he is the true hero!'

"The star was cunning. It said, 'I am indeed your noble hero, please free me!'

"The hero gave the star a secret smile, and then ran. Half the ancient people pursued, and the other half hastened to free the person they thought was their hero. The star was yet still cunning, it said, 'I will chase down the imposter! Leave it to me!' And it gave chase. The two heroes ran about the city, each claiming to be chasing the other.

"The hero, that is, the true hero, stopped at his house to rest. He hid, and watched through his doorway. The city calmed. The star was still wandering about, but he assured everyone that he had chased the imposter right out of the city. In truth, he was still searching, but without frenzy. He walked around, fearful at the civilization before him, fearful of getting found out.

"Finally, the star noticed the hero in his doorway, beckoning to him. The star approached, and the hero pulled him inside. The hero fed the star, and told him to journey out of the city and return to his home. The star told him, 'I need energy.' The hero was not sure what to give him apart from food, so he pondered for a moment, and gave him water to drink.

"The star left the city, under the guise of the hero, and returned to the skies. They say that the star still looks down on the hero in thanks, and that the hero still looks up as well.

"Supposedly, it's the hero that passed this story down to his children, and to the next generation." Chloe finished.

Yaska, usually stoic, had become quite surprised.

Jan said, "Are you the same star?!"

"No." The Starman said.

Chloe grinned, "So, if the legend is true, and my father says it is, all we have to do is feed the star!"

Jan shook his head, "I apologize, but we already tried. It did not work, he said that our food was not star food."

Chloe looked from Yaska to Jan, and then back to the Starman. She considered Jan's words for a long time. Their food is not star food. The hero's food was. Did that mean that the problem was that Plainkind food specifically was not star food? What was different about what the Plainkind ate, compared to what the hero ate? And then Chloe remembered the odd quirk in Plainkind diet that separated them from nearly every other culture.

"I know what it is!" Chloe stood up, "I think I know what we need to feed the star in order to give him the energy he needs!'

By now the various villagers that had been listening to Chloe's story returned to their responsibilities. Only Jan, Yaska, and the Starman remained around the dwindling fire. Now that the story had turned to discussion, they stood, forming a small circle around the dwindling fire.

"What did the hero give the star in my father's legend?" Chloe asked.

Yaska half-frowned at Chloe, "you said it was just food and drink. We gave him food and drink on the mountain."

"I know, but, like you said, it wasn't star food."

"Well then what is star food?"

Chloe smiled, "Well, what is a star? Here's a better question: the sun is a star, so what is the sun?"

Jan looked into the sky and stared at the sun. His Plainkind eyes adjusted and tried to focus. After a few seconds, he looked away and rubbed his eyes.

"Well, it's bright!" Jan laughed.

Chloe frowned.

Yaska said, "It is bright, and it gives off heat during the day."

"Right, so...?" Chloe questioned.

"So, is the sun a fire?"

"Yes!"

"So stars are made of fire."

"Right!" Chloe clapped her hands together, "Stars are made of fire."

"So we need to figure out what feeds a fire, and feed it to the Starman," Yaska concluded.

"Exactly."

The Starman nodded.

Jan said, "So we have to feed him shrubs and brambles?" He looked at the pile of desert plants he had gathered for the night fire with confusion.

"If I needed to eat shrubs, I would have told you. I learned the word for that." The Starman said.

Chloe laughed, "Don't worry, I'll tell you! Stars don't burn wood or shrubs, you can't grow those things in the sky anyway. Instead they burn hydrogen, carbon, and even iron."

Yaska listened with interest, but Jan said, "They burn what?"

"Hydrogen, for one. It's invisible and flammable," Chloe said, "and a star doesn't really burn it. Instead, it causes a nuclear reaction that combines four hydrogen atoms into beryllium*. At least, that's what the Sol-Metch researchers say. But really, they know more about fission than fusion."

Jan said, "You completely lost me."

Yaska said, "You mostly lost me. But more importantly, do you know where we can get hydrogen?"

Chloe smiled, "Oh, it's in water, and the Plainkind do not drink water, do they." Chloe picked her waterskin up from the ground. "You can separate the hydrogen from the rest of the compound by, ah," Chloe frowned, "running an electric current through it."

Jan and the Starman stared, but Yaska's face showed deadened recognition, "An electric current? Is that not related to the, ah, psyche in Solune culture?"

"Ah, all of our nerves run on electric signals, so creating one outside of a body is..." Chloe trailed off and twiddled her thumbs, "ah, even if it wasn't such a touchy area, how would we even..." Chloe gave up on her whole sentence. She had the water, but she wasn't sure how she could separate it, or even how.

The Starman looked from Yaska to Chloe, and then to Jan. He could see that Jan was unsure of what was going on, but was aware that this was some sort of road block and that they had to do something with Chloe's water. The Starman said, "But, if we are to believe your story then does that not mean that, like the star hero, I can just drink the water?"

Chloe's eyes widened, she brightly said, "of course! Perhaps you can do it within you! Let's at least give it a shot."

She handed the skin to the Starman, who drank a bit. He said, "This is what I needed."

To Chloe's relief, the Starman finished only half the water. He said, "Thank you, you were right, this is star food. I think I should return outside the village."

The Starman started walking towards the place where he had landed. The group followed. As they walked, the sky began to get dark.

Chloe said, "It was quite interesting to meet a star, I would have liked to learn more about you."

Yaska said, "Well, perhaps he can stay."

The Starman shook his head, "You are all quite friendly, but I prefer my own home."

The Starman closed his eyes and began generating energy. His legs slowly morphed away. His body dropped and began to hover above the ground. Then the rest of his features began to lose their form and he, once again, became a ball of light. The star rose up just as other stars began to appear in the darkening sky.

Yaska tried to see which star he would become, but through the dusk and the shimmering atmosphere, it was hard to tell. Jan departed shortly after to make sure the village had a fire, and Chloe and Yaska were left alone, watching.

"Did you see which star he was?" Yaska said.

Chloe said, "It's hard to tell. To be honest, I don't really know the locations of the stars. They're hard to see in the Solune Kingdom too, so we don't really engage in mapping them."

"Oh. He was a little strange. Silent. Perhaps he did not particularly enjoy our company."

"He must have had some reason for wanting to get home. For all we know, that could be the reason for his coldness. Maybe stars just think differently than us." Chloe shrugged and sat on the sand. Yaska sat next to her.

"I wonder," Yaska said, "If that star in your story wanted to stay."

"Well, my father says he did. I guess, like us, stars have individual differences too."

Yaska considered her words. She thought about Chloe's father. She had met him, the Solune King, before. He was said to be immortal.

Yaska said, "Was your father the hero from the story?"

Chloe turned her head and smiled, "I think so." She shook her head, and added, "He told me that the star might return at some point."

"Is it afraid of taking the form of someone influential again? Or getting attacked?"

"Yeah," Chloe continued, "Hey, let's go visit the fire. Maybe Jan will have a new story for us."

"Or maybe you could give us another of yours." Yaska said warmly.

They both smiled, and returned to the village together. Chloe did end up telling another story. She did not say it, but it about the same hero. Here, she simply called him the King.

Notes:

*The Sol-Metch researchers are incorrect about this. In basic terms, s star will fuse two hydrogen atoms into a helium, and then later will fuse two helium atoms into beryllium. The Sol-Metch and Solune scientific communities have not yet discovered helium, and so at the moment they assume that hydrogen either fuses by threes into lithium, or by fours into beryllium.

Alice and Finch – Chapter 13: Sluggish Mind

"No, you'll have to try again, dear." The old woman said.

"Ah! Ahh!" Growls of anger drifted from between clenched teeth.

Then the splintering of wood was heard.

Oritha had switched very quickly from pens to pencils. Alice frequently became frustrated, and when things were had gotten particularly foul, she often snapped them. Oritha had lost a somewhat expensive fountain pen to this, followed by profuse apology. Now it was clear that a small investment into a bulk order of one hundred inexpensive pencils was a wise decision. This girl had uncanny strength. At least, it would be uncanny if her arms and legs didn't bulge so, proving such strength to be quite canny.

"Why am I having so really stupid!" Alice shouted, mashing the pencil tip into the table as if it were no stronger than a blade of grass.

"Dear, I have told you over and over. You are not stupid, you are just a slow learner. You are a natural at physical tasks, but not at mental ones."

Then Oritha stopped and considered her statement. Upon reflection, she realized that it was not true. Recounting their years' worth of lessons, Oritha concluded that Alice had never forgotten a thing she had learned. Her final examinations were identical in score to her earlier preparatory tests. It was as if information was encoded far more thoroughly into her mind.

"That is actually incorrect. You just learn differently than everyone else."

"What is that supposed to mean? Drake said that that's what teachers tell their stupid students to make them feel better." Alice retorted.

"Drake is correct about that," Oritha admitted, "I have told students such for those reasons before I retired."

"Ah-ha!" Alice accused.

"What did I tell you about 'ah-ha,' Alice?" Oritha responded calmly?

"That, I should stop saying it because I always immediately get proven wrong?" Alice responded in what had once been Oritha's own words.

"Yes. So, in most cases I was correct, in that some such students had successful futures outside of academia. No, I mean it in your case. Answer me this, what are the four major cities in Murdock? The ones to which the surrounding settlements and villages pay taxes, and from which they take rulings?"

Alice wasn't sure what was happening, but she answered her teacher, "By population, Hannibal, M-Murdock, Baracus, and FACE. But FACE doesn't have any proxy settlements."

Oritha was impressed, but not surprised that Alice had remembered the point on FACE.

"And the Capital?"

"Is Murdock. That's where from I have."

"Try again."

"It is Murdock, isn't it?" Alice asked, but then realized her syntax issue, "Oh, That's where I am from!"

"Okay," Oritha decided to give her a more difficult one.

It was something they had learned at the beginning. Alice had wanted to learn nearly everything about Murdock.

"What are the names of the members of the Royal Family?"

"Why are you asking me all this?"

"Do you not know?" Oritha asked, adding, "I will explain after, dear."

"The wife of the King is called Gwenhime, she had no last name, and so she took his, Rhye. Then, from youngest to oldest is Chloe, Janna, Natasha and Kain are twins, Zealott, and Crystal Jealousy. We don't know the King's name, do we?"

"No we do not." Oritha nodded, but then Alice continued.

"Right, but his nickname is Mars. He has two brothers, also unnamed, but called Pluto and Venus. Pluto has a wife called On'hor who is thought to be a spirit, their children are called Gaul and Millie."

Oritha was taken aback.

"I did not teach you any of that," She said.

"No, I read about it. Drake gave me a book." Alice said.

"Oh. Well, still this proves my point. Most students had forgotten most of the names after this much time had passed. And yet, you haven't!" Oritha said proudly.

"What... What by that do are you saying?"

"Try again." Oritha said once more.

Alice cleared her throat, and her mind, "What do you mean by that?"

"Consider the wood carver." Oritha started.

Alice listened intently.

"He makes a sign with letters carved very shallow into it. It only takes a day to make it. The rains and the sands batter it, and in a few months, what happens?"

"The maybe sign it," Alice saw Oritha's look and tried again, "The sign maybe fades?"

"Right! But consider a second wood carver. This woman carves deep, meaningful letters into their board. It takes many days to complete, but when it is finished how long do you think it lasts?"

"Years!" Alice jumped up, causing the house to shudder.

"Please sit down. What have I told you about jumping? You are nearly two hundred pounds now, and only fifteen. I would not want you falling through the floor, dear."

"Oh, sorry," Alice sat, "but that's me? I the second carver is what I will are to be?"

Her sentences got worse when she was excited or angry. Oritha gave her another look.

Alice sighed, "I am the second carver?"

Oritha nodded sagely. She reached back and removed her black hairpin, letting her long grey hair fall around her shoulders. Alice recognized this as the signal that class was nearly over.

"You have a very good memory for what you have learned, but in order to etch that memory, you have to carve deeper. It's not that you have a sluggish mind, but rather a deliberate memory. Please, try to be patient with yourself as I have been patient with you."

"Yes miss." Alice nodded.

"Now, you have a good evening. Don't let your father, sorry, your second father work you too hard. I don't need you coming here sore again."

It seemed that every time Alice had come to her house sore, her muscles had become noticeably larger. Oritha was almost tempted to start measuring her arm's circumference.

That's probably what I'll teach tomorrow, she thought, circles.

It wasn't just that. Alice had grown quite a bit since she had first arrived. Before, Alice had been an adorable little creature with a permanently joyful grimace. Now, that grimace was beginning to realize that there was more than one emotion. Alice was hitting adolescence.

There wasn't a lot of information on Plainkind development, but Oritha was sure that this seemingly late development was quite on time. Alice had grown physically too. It seemed that, possibly reacting to the work, her shoulders had broadened. Oritha had read this somewhere, that the twin Y shaped spine of the Plainkind would broaden to adapt and increase strength and leverage.

Finally, Alice had become lanky. She wasn't quite tall, but she had certainly grown. Over a cubit in fact! No longer was she small waist high girl, now she reached chest or shoulder height. Oritha had noted that Alice had more the physique of a young athletic man. Not the stocky build of a worker, but the lean, flexible build of a courier or a hunter.

Yes, she had a very masculine torso. But her face was still quite beautiful and feminine. Perhaps more so, now that she was starting to look less like an excited cherub and more like a high-spirited woman.

Alice and Finch – Chapter 19: Plains Woman

With trembling hand, Alice crossed out the last day on her calendar. She had had her birthday just yesterday, but she hadn't told anyone. She didn't want to create a fuss the day before she left.

She had told Jithin a while ago that she was going to leave soon, and when she climbed down her ladder with a backpack on, he was waiting for her.

He said, "I am going with you."

Alice had not been expecting this, "Don't worry, I am an adult now. I turned nineteen just yesterday."

Jithin's brow furrowed. He started counting on his fingers.

"Alice, you're only fifteen or sixteen in adjusted Solune years. The Plainkind don't reach maturity until the age of twenty-one."

Alice blushed, and pushed her fists down at her side, "Well I used to live on my own just fine!"

Jithin gave her a sort of pleading, imploring look.

She shook her head, "You can move to Murdock with me if you want. But! I am not going to wait for you! I have to get back as soon as possible. I have an appointment."

"That calendar?"

Alice nodded. Before she could leave, four men and a woman entered the little house. Alice knew these people; it was Jithin's work crew.

"Hello, Workhorse, we heard you were leaving today!" One of them said.

"Yes!" The woman said, "I talked to the owner of the Keeper. We're throwing you a party. A goodbye party!"

"Ah!" Alice smiled.

She wasn't sure why, but the woman had brought a suitcase with her. When they entered the Keeper, all of Alice's Militia were already there, along with Oritha and Drake. They cheered for her.

Alice milled about, excitedly saying her goodbyes and telling everyone about her plans to return to her childhood friends, and about Finch. She told the story of how Finch had helped her so many times, she was sure everyone had heard it twice.

Then, as Alice was describing Finch's hair to Oritha, the woman from Jithin's crew slammed her suitcase on the table. Oritha jumped, and Alice turned to stare at her.

"What is all that, Arihanna?" Alice asked her.

Arihanna crossed her arms, "You're three and a half cubits tall, right? So am I. It's clothes."

Alice heard clapping behind her. A few of the militia cheered.

She heard one say, "Yeah, dress her up!"

Jithin called out too, "You don't want to be wearing work clothes when you meet up with your boyfriend!"

Alice looked down at her brown coveralls. She didn't really care, but after all, it couldn't hurt to arrive looking pretty. She blushed a little.

"Oh." She said in a small voice.

Arihanna smiled at her and busted open the trunk. She pulled out a green dress.

"There are no legs," Alice said.

"That's the point. It looks cute," Arihanna replied.

Alice looked around, frowning. She didn't want to wear such a stupid looking article no matter how cute it was supposed to look.

"I want something I can climb in without showing my underwear," Alice stated.

Arihanna had realized that the dress was not impressing Alice, and so she threw it aside. "Green doesn't work for you anyway."

Oritha watched all this, as they were sitting at her table. She said, "I'm sure you'll find that Alice's colour is orange."

Arihanna nodded and dug. She pulled out an orange dress. It was very short, the kind of thing you wear if you really want to show off more thigh.

Alice noticed, and turned a little pink. Arihanna handed it to Alice, and then found a pair of white capris, and handed those to her too.

"Oh," Alice said again.

"Well, go to the washroom and-" But Alice had already changed clothes before she finished.

"Hmm?" Alice asked.

"Well then!" Arihanna said, "Look at this! It's perfect! Turn around, Alice."

Alice did a little spin as Jithin came to the table and sat down next to Oritha.

"It looks great!" He said.

"Just one thing." One of Jithin's crew had followed him. It was a very slick and beautiful Riley man whom Alice knew to be called Elliot.

He pushed his greased hair further back and took off his taupe-white scarf and proceeded to wrap it around Alice's waist. Then, he tied a large beautiful bow at her back. He double knotted it so that it wouldn't undo, no matter how far she ran. Elliot was quite aware of how rough Alice was.

Elliot pushed Alice's chest, "Child, you have no chest and your hips are small. The only thing you have going for you is your slim waist."

Alice's face burned, turning from pink to red.

She said simply, "Oh."

Arihanna piped up, "Well, she has a pretty face too!"

Elliot crossed his arms, "Yes, but she's not about to put clothing on her face. Actually..."

Elliot reached across and took the hair clip out of Arihanna's hair. Arihanna also blushed. The clip had a silver flower on it.

"Is this not a desert lily?" He asked.

"Yeah, it is. Yes." Arihanna stammered.

Alice swayed a little as she watched them. She wondered if they were going to start dating after she left. Probably.

Elliot noticed her stare, "That is perfect! A desert flower for our desert prince."

He tied Alice's hair back.

"Oh!"

Arihanna pulled a mirror from her suitcase. It was so large that Alice wondered how it had fit. She saw herself. She tilted her head left, then right, then she swayed and twisted. She clapped her hands together.

"Wonderful!" She said, "But, I can't take all these things from you..."

Oritha spoke now, "Alice, dear, was it not your birthday only yesterday?"

Elliot clapped, "Happy birthday, Alice!"

It seemed that her game of dress-up had become a sort of exhibition because the rest of the inn had heard them. They all chorused happy birthday, cheering. Oritha nodded her approval.

As things began to wind down, Alice waved goodbye to everyone.

She leaned in to Arihanna and whispered, "You and Elliot should start a clothing store."

And then she promptly exited.

Alice stopped at Main Street, realizing that there was a small group following her. It was Jithin, Oritha, and Drake.

"Dear, your schooling is not yet complete!" Oritha cried.

Alice looked down to her feet. "There are more important things for me to do."

Oritha nodded sombrely.

Drake said, "I'm coming too. I need to meet up with Janna about the guards here."

"So Baracus will be safe without me?" Alice asked.

"Yeah. Haven't you seen? Murdock and Hannibal have both sent over those willing to relocate. We just need a formal Captain and Vice-Captain." After hearing this, a weight lifted from her shoulders.

Jithin entered the square. Alice shook hands and gave out unlimited hugs. She was shorter than everyone, but also stronger.

Alice took a deep breath and stared off in the distance towards Murdock.

"It's four-hundred kilocubits away. That's a five day walk, if we walk eight hours." Drake said to her.

Alice did a very slow calculation. Her brain was not good with maths, it was good with facts. Recollection.

Four-hundred kilocubits divided by five days. Eighty kilocubits per day. She had to keep track of her units or else she would be lost at the end. Okay, eighty divided by eight is ten. That's ten per hour. And what was her top speed? Not sprinting, jogging. Alice wasn't sure. She guessed forty kilocubits per hour. Four hundred divided by forty. Ten.

"I'll be there in ten hours." She said after nearly five minutes of calculation.

"What?" This made absolutely zero sense to Drake.

Alice turned to her second father, and to Oritha, who had become almost a grandmother to her. She waved.

"I'll see you in five days, Alice!" Jithin called.

"Yeah." Alice called. She ran back to him, and reached up. They embraced, and Alice shed a tear.

"Don't worry, Alice, it's only five days."

Alice's heart began to beat with excitement. For her, it was only ten hours. Adrenaline began to leak into her bloodstream, and she figured she had better start using it.

Alice had walked backwards all the way out to the town limits, waving.

She whispered, "It's not goodbye, it's, see you later, Alice. It's time to see Finch. It is later."

She pivoted and began to canter and then jog. Her muscles started to shift again, and before she realized it, her jog had turned to a low-energy sprint. She glided down the path, her bare feet gouging holes in the dirt.

"Woo!"

She stared ahead, and her eyes adjusted. She could see, far far in the distance. Plainkind eyes are almost telescopic. It was one of the many overpowered traits that remained from the days of Birth.

Alice had been right. It only took her ten hours to cross the four hundred kilocubit bridge between her and her destination. Before she knew it, Alice was at the outer walls of Murdock catching her breath.

Alice and Finch: Archetypal Recapitulation

Nine months ago [as of Winter 2018], I powered through the first chapter of a three-part short story series. That series is what later became the "Dawn" section of Alice and Finch. It was a very strong trilogy compared to my other work, and it eventually spawned my current best piece of writing, Inck. But then, three months later in late July, I finally finished the first draft of the novel. After that, I started tying up loose ends with a few epilogues, and I also realized major a flaw. As I looked back, I realized that I hadn't really finished the story properly.

According to Canadian literary theorist Northrop Frye, "The theme of the comic is the integration of society, which usually takes the form of incorporating a central character into it" (Frye). The integration can be broken down into individual, family, and society. I'm not so sure that I succeeded in this regard, but I think I made a good effort. In fact, in my own epilogue for Ilias, I somehow managed to subconsciously notice my own mistakes! Here's a clipping with a limit on spoilers:

> *Ilias came up with something of "... a solution neither Finch nor Alexandre had thought of ..." (Triumph).*

This is an example of one of the many loose ends that I want to tie up; not in the band-aid epilogues, but in the actual story.

Northrop Frye's, "The Anatomy of Criticism, Third Essay: Archetypal Criticism"

Northrop Frye is pretty cool. As far as I know, he took Aristotle's theory of Comedy and Tragedy and expanded on it. I'm currently taking a Greek Literature course and, apparently almost all ancient Novels were... romance novels. Specifically, in the category of

Greek Comedy. Here's a few things that I accidentally stumbled on that qualify my *Alice and Finch* as an almost-archetypal comedy.

Next is the character types he talks about. There are four types of characters in the comic plot, but two of them are mostly used in drama to play to the audience, so I'm leaving those ones out. The two main types are the eiron and the alazon. Eiron characters are helpful characters, protagonists, sidekicks, and other "self-deprecating" allies, as Frye puts it. Self-deprecating in this context essentially means is that they recognise, somehow, that the main character is "more important" than they are, and are very much okay with helping them sometimes even to their own detriment. Alazons are 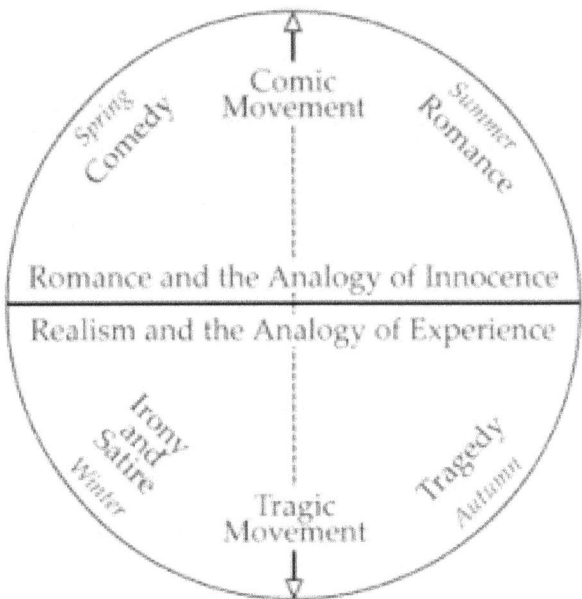 unhelpful characters. Not necessarily antagonists, but I'll get to that after. Alazon characters are, essentially, anyone who gets in the way of the main characters getting together and having their happy ending.

I've also noticed that in these ancient Greek novels, the title is often the names of the two main characters. *Chaereas and Callirhoe, Daphnis and Chloe, Leucippe and Clitophon, Metiochus and Parthenope, Alice and Finch*... interesting.

My Characters, and some Deviations from Archetypes

Let's make a chart.

Eiron
- Finch (Protagonist)
- Alice (Protagonist)
- Jutt (Sidekick)
- Artus (Sidekick)
- Chloe (Self-Deprecating*)
- Jithin & Oritha (Self-Deprecating)
- Bat (Benevolent Father*)

Alazon
- Ilias, Finch's father (Father)
- Jutt (????, potential rival*)
- Guard (Blocking)
- Captain (Blocking)

*Anything with a star indicates a deviation from the archetype.

Eirons

Alice Dawngale and Finch Dirge Zeth.

According to Frye, the protagonist eiron characters tend to be bland, and not that unique. I would argue that Finch and Alice are fairly unique and interesting; they have specific interests and goals, and unique personalities. Finch might be too prodigal for his own good, but at least he's not a creative genius on top of it all. Alice came from the sky, is an outside, almost unheard of race, and she's upbeat and excitable. You might argue that she's too feminine, but she's got an almost militant optimism, and immense physical strength due to her ancestry. Actually, she also struggles learning in class, which is a more masculine issue. What I'm arguing, is that I've failed to have bland eiron protagonists to fit the Greek standard. I'm okay with that.

Alexandre "Jutt" Dirge.

Jutt falls into the sidekick category quite nicely, in fact, almost perfectly. She helps Finch out, and is the one he talks to about his problems. And, she's also self-deprecating. Although, her "self-deprecation" is due less to comic structure, and more to the fact that she's resigned to her own life and future. I'm hoping to write her story, but... it's really difficult. I've already failed twice.

Artus Zephophile.

Artus doesn't start off as a sidekick, but you could make a case that he becomes one as the two join the guard and train together. Also, I'll note here that it's more common for male protagonists to have sidekicks than females. (Although *An Ephesian Tale* reverses this.) Before that Artus is Finch's best friend, so that's something.

Chloe Rhye, fifth Prince of the Solune.

Okay, so Chloe is a clear eiron / helping character. She's not really self-deprecating, but she does take time out of her... not that busy day to teach Finch. And I maybe some other people too, but I can't remember if I actually wrote that in.

Jithin and Oritha.

These two are the clear helping characters for Alice. Not much to say about it. You could argue that they're self-deprecating; Jithin actually goes through the resources and cost of housing and feeding Alice, and the Plainkind are nearly obligate carnivores, so that's no joke. Oritha takes the effort to teach Alice too.

Alazon

Ilias Zeth.

Finch's father Ilias is almost entirely archetypal in his comic role. He's the "angry father figure that gets in the way of the lovers" type character. I think the big difference is that he's not really getting in the way because he doesn't want them to be married.

It's more... paranoia, or closed mindedness. Also, he seems to have his own character arc for some reason. I'm not sure how I managed that.

Alexandre "Jutt" Dirge.

Might as well talk about Jutt here. So, in the current draft of the story Jutt is hinted as being a romantic rival for Finch. It is a little weird, seeing as they're cousins and neither are all that interested. (You could argue that as recently as the nineteenth century cousins were still marrying, though the term "cousin" was also used to refer to second and third cousins, so the research may be murky.) Alexandre grows up to be a cold, violent, and ambivalent sort of person in her adolescence before growing up into a scholarly housewife. In *Alice and Finch* we see these elements in their earliest stages; Alexandre is something of a trickster figure. I'm not really sure if I'm going to leave this loose interaction in later drafts. It was put in as a tension device, but I might be able to do better. We'll see once I hit the planning phase.

The Guard and the Captain.

"The Guard" is one of many people who want Alice out of the city because she's different. He, with the help of his grouchy Captain, are the ones who conspire to get her arrested and locked away, and are the catalyst for Alice's self-imposed exile. Very standard Alazon "blocking character" activity here. Although, again, like with Ilias, it isn't about stopping a marriage. In fact, these two may be more unorthodox in regards to archetypes than I realize.

I'll explain. See, generally the people who cause the pair of comic lovers to split up or leave their home are **pirates!** They'll generally capture the woman, or both the man and the woman, and sell them as slaves. Pirates are a double representation of chaos, as far as I can tell. They are outside of the standard system, and they live on the ocean. That's two chaotic things. So I'm not sure what it means that the blocking characters in *Alice and Finch* are part of the society already. Maybe it's another element of the "flawed society that needs to be mended at the end" as Frye might put it. The guards are a representation of the corrupt parts of the **society** that need to be fixed or removed for the final reintegration. (Although, I guess Diesel and her gang are decent stand-ins for pirates.)

Separation

The separation of the two main characters in a Comic plot is pretty much mandatory, so I guess I checked that box.

What else. Okay, there should be a flaw at the **personal, familial,** and **societal** levels. Anything wrong with Finch? Not really, outside of the fact that he's incapable of helping Alice. And, he's insufficient as a child when it comes to that task, so he could use some improvement. What about Alice? Well, I'm coming to the conclusion that I need to explore Alice a little more. Right now, there isn't much wrong with her, outside the fact that she is a slow learner. (Ha! Mary Sue has been closley avoided! Really, this is the one weakness of the Plainkind. They're just so much better at so many things haha.)

How about his **family**? Well Ilias is a blocking character, so yes. How about **society**? Well, this is a society that is discriminatory, and the court and guards are conspiring together, so it's definitely flawed, as I discussed above.

The Reintegration and the Antagonists

I'll go through the three levels again.

Individual.

Well, both Alice and Finch improve immensely by the end of the novel. Finch becomes a high-ranking guard, and Alice gets educated and becomes something of a local hero. So, everyone's pulling their weight. **Familial** level? Well, in the epilogue anyway, (and this needs to be moved into the actual text) Ilias drops the charges, so there's the integration of the family. Jutt... well, she actually gets a tragic ending as far as this draft is concerned. It's meant to set her up for a sequel, and really, this isn't the place for her story anyway. Poor Jutt.

Society?

Definitely. The corrupt Captain character gets replaced, or retires or something. And, there is a sort of party! They destroy the church of Conflict... as weird as that sounds. It actually might be accidentally symbolic, the conflict is over and the main characters are now able to live "happily ever after." (I'll tell you a secret; marriage has its own difficulties.)

Laying out Frye's Theory of Structuralism as it Manifests in Alice and Finch

So, Alice and Finch checks enough boxes to be engaging and recognisable as an archetypal Comedy, but it's unique enough to be its own thing. And, some of the uniqueness actually helps the overall message. At least, that's what I, the author, would like to think.

I'll add that the major deviation I've made is that the main characters start off as children, and grow into young adults by the end. This must be what changes the motivations of the alazon characters from breaking up a romance, to getting rid of Alice.

Themes and Sub-Themes

This is getting rather long, so I'll keep my discussion of themes limited for now. So far, here are the themes that I could recognise from editing the first three chapters.

- Education
- Sacrificing in the Present for the Future
- Growing up / Coming of age in the Classical / Archaic (not modern) sense
- Outsiders and how they fit in

This may have been my primal or logical brain subconsciously directing my work, but Alice and Finch are young, and they're constantly being educated. Finch is taught by his father, and then Prince Chloe (somehow), whereas Alice is taught by Finch, and then Oritha. I'm not sure to what effect this education leads, but I think it's necessary, normal, and relatable for children to be educated, so don't expect it to be edited out. Sacrificing the present for the future. This is one of the most powerful messages in human history, as far as I can tell. People who retire rich generally do so by saving. That is, sacrificing current wealth for future gain. It's investing; investing in your future. So, the point of sacrifice actually connects to the other theme of education. The big, obvious sacrifice, of course, is Finch's. He derails his future of higher education in order to become a guard and help Alice. That's real commitment. Does Alice do anything back? Has she suffered enough already? I'm not sure, I'll have to look into that in the next draft.

Finally, and this might be the biggest sub-theme, there's outsiders. I was reading this and I couldn't believe all the wierdos I'd put in my story! Alice is obviously an unusual creature, as a Plainkind. Finch is also a minority, being a Riley instead of a Solune. The only majority child is Artus, and he's regrettably average.

As for a major theme, I think it's obviously the Comic plot; getting the two main characters back together by the end, and reintegrating them with society.

The Youth of Yaska May Däwngale

    I idealized my older sister. I would follow her everywhere. During a hunt, I would follow her, keeping quiet. She would talk when no prey was around. She spoke of the mountains north, the Solune kingdom east, and sometimes of a kingdom lost in the desert storm to the west. I took only minor interest. I preferred the hunt, not these foreign places. My sister, Reyla, proved through these conversations that she felt the opposite. On one hunt she said to me, "When you can take up this post as your own, I will likely leave it behind myself." I was devastated; was she planning on leaving me? I would worry of this overnights, while the two of us slept in our bed. Reyla had been my sole caretaker for as long as I could remember. She spent a lot of time with Jan who also helped take care of me. Would she leave me with him? Or wait until I was an adult myself?

    Years passed, and my worries faded.

    Then one morning our village was hit by a sandstorm. Reyla shook me awake, telling me to run toward the east, toward the Solune wall. I did. I do not question my sister's judgement. She helped nearly everyone out of the village, Jan and her together. When the homes finally got hit, she was there, with my very young friend Marisa. Reyla pulled her from the stone brick house and bodily threw her to us. Jan ran to help, and caught the flying child, and did everything he could to shield her from the fall. Reyla ran toward us yelling for us to run, run!

    Before she could finish her third shout, she was taken by the sandstorm. Everyone except me heeded her calls. I stood there, looking at the swirling sands before me. I searched for her with my eyes, I searched for me dear sister as the storm drew closer.

Jan ran, still carrying Marisa. He took me up in his other arm and ran. I did not resist him. I was not stupid.

We never found her buried in the sands. She did end up leaving after all, but not how she had wanted.

WHAT WAS IT LIKE? THE FUTURE.

"WHAT WAS IT LIKE? THE FUTURE."
"I could see myself, lifting things that I could not touch."
"COULD NOT TOUCH?"
"Yes, I could move things that were far away, I could...control matter as I pleased. It was...frightening."
"YOU ARE NOT THE CHOSEN ONE, AND YET YOU HAVE THEIR POWER."
"The...their power?"

"YOU ARE THE CURSED ONE, YOU ARE THE SATAN. WE MUST KILL YOU. WE MUST KILL YOU SO THAT THE CHOSEN CAN TAKE BACK THE POWER. YOU ARE NOT THE CHOSEN!"

"Kill me? What? What...what if I am the CHOSEN?" She said.

The Shriken Elder's face became fierce. It was a look that Yaska was used to. All the Shriken people were the same in this respect. They had three pronged pupils, many long, sharp molars, and a they could pull their cheeks back, just like the Plainkind, in order to let their mouths open wider.

That is what the Elder was doing. He bared his maw and brandished his claws. His giant leathery wings unfurled, and he swept himself forward, driving his knee into her.

Yaska was knocked to the ground. She stood and clawed at the man, but nothing happened. His skin was harder than stone. She drew her sword from the metal clasp on her back and cut across. The man did not flinch, he simply walked towards her slowly.

"Why are you attacking me?"

The Elder said, "YOU ARE NOT THE CHOSEN, BUT YOU WILL HAVE THE POWER. THIS IS NOT ALLOWED, YOU HAVE TAKEN IT."

A young woman appeared in doorway holding a Plainkind medical knife.

Yaska stepped away from him, backpedaling until her she was against the wall. She looked left and right. She saw a square hole; a window.

The Elder was slow, Yaska knew it was because he was cursed, and suffered from grinding bones in both knees. He would get over it in a few years; the Plainkind were immune to chronic illness. But for now, the man edged towards her, death in his eyes.

Yaska turned left and dived out of the hole. She opened her own wings, small and deformed, and dropped to the ground with jagged grace; plummeting. This place, this ancient Shriken temple, was built into the mountain that overlooked the Plainkind desert. It overlooked the rolling hills of sand and its inhabitants, the Plainkind and the dinosaurs. They were all Plainkind, even the Shriken, but the older race liked to pretend they were better.

From within the building, the Elder shrieked. The sound cut the air, travelling hundreds of kilocubits.

This is mountain where they watched the youth survive.

Yaska could see them, the Shriken people, heeding the Elder's call. They soared through the sky towards the mountain.

"Oh no…"

Yaska didn't know what she was going to do. She didn't think she could take out an entire settlement's worth of them.

She turned around to see if she could find refuge back in the mountain, but stone door was sealed.

Yaska ran to it and started knocking, her fist creating deep seated cracks in gate with each hit, but it was not enough. She frantically looked around. The Shriken were getting close. They seemed to cover the sky. Where was the elder? He had not followed. Who was in the crowd?

She saw someone flying in front of them; it was her older sister, Reyla. What, was she coming for the kill as well?

The first of the Shriken landed. She looked around and saw her sister's back.

"Run!" Reyla shouted. She held a ten foot wooden pole and began beating her companions with it.

Yaska threw herself through the damaged door and turned back. Reyla had subdued three or four of them, Yaska couldn't tell exactly.

"Go! Do not worry about me. The would not kill another Shiken. Hey," she paused for a moment and turned, "are you really the CHOSEN ONE?"

"I do no think so—they want to kill me because I stole the CHOSEN'S powers!"

"What nonsense. Go now!" Reyla pushed her stick against a group of attackers and stepped forward. She walked, shoving more and more against the dull pole, and then she swung. The wood strained, but Reyla successfully managed to fling a small group of her attackers across and into the air.

Yaska spun and ran into the temple. She was inside a wide open stadium, and was immediately confronted with the Elder. She looked around past him, her eyes cutting the dark environment. She saw the hall that followed the mountain's circumference and dashed, pulling her wings out and down a touch so that they helped, rather than hindered, her running. Her gait was one step above a run, maintaining a glide by launching herself forward with each stride.

The entire temple was black, because the Plainkind could see in the dark. Various limbs and bladed weapons crashed through the wall, coming in from outside. Yaska knew that they were locating her by vibration. Most of them missed, but Yaska also collected a few scrapes and cuts from the odd sword that hit true. She ran down the claustrophobic tube for three, then four strides before she was confronted by another person; the woman with the knife.

"Ah, wait!" Yaska skidded to a stop, her clawed feet digging into the stone.

"No, we are done waiting, you will stop now."

Yaska was thrust into the wall. The Elder's hands grabbed her, blasting through the stone wall behind her. Yaska was caught in his hold. She was held around the waist by the Elder, and pinned by the shoulder by the woman.

She said, "The knife," and then handed it over.

The man punched a hole for his head with his off hand, and Yaska squirmed beneath the woman's pin.

"What are you?" Yaska looked around. The attacks from outside had stopped, and she wondered if it was due to her capture, or if perhaps Reyla had defeated them all.

The Elder forced his torso through the wall, and stone crumbled around him.

"No!" Yaska moved her shoulders. The woman dug her fingers into Yaska's body until she drew blood.

"Yes. It is what must be done."

"No!"

The Elder stabbed the knife into Yaska's left thigh, and then slowly drew it up her body. It cut deep, deep past the nerves. For the most part, Yaska did not feel it. It was all too deep. She gasped, in and out of adrenaline shock. He cut upward, nicking her ribs as he went, cutting the upper edge of her right breast, and then up the shoulder.

Yaska looked down and watched as the think line of pink blood slowly turned red.

When he had reached the top of her shoulder, the Elder continued around it and down her back.

"No!"

Yaska's heart began to pump faster, and for a few beats blood squirted out of the long incision. She gritted her teeth and forcibly pulled the laceration shut by the specialized sinews.

"No!"

Her eyes glowed red, and she looked into the maroon eyes of the woman.

"NO!"

With raw strength, Yaska pulled free of both sets of hands and grabbed the young woman's face in her hand. She slammed her head into the outer wall, cracking it along it's length. Then she did it again, and the poor Shriken was launched into the hot desert air, no longer conscious. Yaska's wound was still oozing, but it greatly inhibited by the sheer force of her clenching sinews and muscles.

"YOU MUST DIE FOR THE GREATER GOOD!" The Elder said.

Yaska spun to face him, "THE GREATER GOOD WILL BE THE DOWNFALL OF YOUR CIVILIZATION."

The Elder's expression became fierce; murderous. He stepped forward and thrust the sword into Yaska's heart.

One pump emptied the organ of it's blood. It splattered across the elder's torso. Yaska stared, eyes wide open.

"YOU CANNOT KILL..." Yaska spoke, as though in another language. Words came out, as if she was speaking as written text. "YOU CANNOT KILL THAT WHICH IS ETERNAL."

She took his hand and stabbed him with the knife he still held. The Elder stood in shock, his own hand, his own knife piercing his chest. The Elder died.

Then, Yaska fell on top of him.

"Wah!" Reyla turned her sister over and looked at the wound.

It had healed, leaving a long scar running across Yaska's body. The younger woman woke up, her head pounding.

"Reyla... did we kill the thief?"

"Kill?"

Yaska's eyes opened. She looked around.

"Are you okay, sister?"

"You are my sister then?" Yaska said.

"Yes, do you not remember?"

"I only remember dying. I remember language, and I remember all my knowledge but... I don't remember any people."

Reyla embraced her sister. "Once more you have abandoned me... Don't worry Yaska. I will take care of you."

grunge

It's dark in here,   Uncomfortable
It feels warm,   It's easy, I sit
I sit and I sit and,   I'm laid-back and
Never sleep right,   Can't quite tell
And I'm dizzy,   But it's warm and
Don't worry about nothing   'Til it's too late and

Then we panic.

A Canto of Alexandre Dirge

I come from a long line of those deceased,
My father, a criminal, for one, when I was very young,
Killed, I am told, on some crime lord's order,
By my mother, to save the family, she told me.
Just her and I, now. And this order of crime.

Where has she gone since?
Gone like her mind,
                  no better than my mind,
Actually quite worse.

I joined them myself after;
tried to save her,
proved my worth,
Fought, kill and then be killed, failed.

Punishments extreme then.
Lost only my teeth, then
                  and ruined them all,
And I set her free.[1]

Escaped, given only a short sentence,
I'd colluded with guards.

Where had mother gone?
She got caught up?
Missing, only
                who knows.

Tried to get an education, didn't last very long though.
I'd journeyed from town, on request from Chloe Rhye, the Solune Prince,°

And even then———hadn't seen mother since.
The young Prince took us to a faraway place, the Lussa, a new nation.
Took my incontinence with me, so I could fall again.

Among the Prince's group,
I met an unpleasant young man,
Which was wonderful for me,
And I was wonderful for him.

We fought a great civil war, in the Lussa City State.
We took back the throne,
                                  from overreaching aristocrats and polits.
I took control of myself,
long enough to give a hand.
And after, I wanted to go off,
                                  start a life with that man.

But like my father before me,
before him, I thought he had died in the end.
Lynched, being on the wrong side.
Saw him hanging in the street,
                                  That's what I had thought,
But the body had gone.

And now I am here.
I have come a long way but,
I felt like I'd lost it all,
I remember my voice from then

... *He's just missing*
... *He's still alive*
... *He's just run away,*
... *He is just missing*
... *He is ...*

Missing or not,
Either way, he has gone.

And now I am indentured here,
I have sold off my time, because,
in a new far off city,

I had given up.

Why is it that I was so good at fatalist thinking?
Why did I let myself be taken so low?
The Djeb City State sprawls around me,
threatening change.
A revolution is here.
A Darker Red.

Here I had given up my life, here I'm decoration, I am a slave.
I feel that I had sold my life. *I had. Had.*
But I opened my eyes,
then opened them again,
        after a year had passed,
So here I begin.

How will I get out of this now—though?
Involuntary arbitration?
My mother came,[2]
       and burned the place down.[3]

And we ran off,
mad women, as we always were.
      And when we had gone,
I thought,

What really happened after the war?
Oh my love—aren't you out there somewhere?[4]

¹See: Raze
²See: Shade the Past
³See: Wraith Hail
°See: The Solune Prince
⁴See: String Quartet

PS Y CHOSIS

```
PPPPPPPPPPPPPPPPPPPPPPPPPPPPPPPPPPPPPPPPPPPPPPPPPP
PPPPPPPPPPPPPPPSSSSSSSSSSSSSSSSSSSSSSPPPPPPPPPPPPPP
PPPPPPPPSSSSSSSSSSYYYYYYYYYYYYYSSSSSSSSSSSPPPPPPPPP
PPPPPPPSSSSSSSSSSSYYYYCCCCCCCYYYYYSSSSSSSSSSSPPPPPPP
PPPPPSSSYYCCCOPPPPSSYYYCHCCOOOOOOOOPSSSYYYCCCOOPPPPPPPP
PPPPPSSYYYCCCOOOPPSSYYYCHCCOOOOOOOOOPSSYYYYCCCOOOOPPPPPP
PPPPPSSYYYCCOOOOPPSSYYYCHCCOOOOOOOOOPSSYYYYCCCOOOOPPPPPP
PPPPSSYYYCCCOOOOOOOSSSIICCCCCCCCCCOOOPSSYYYCCCOOSSIISPPPP
PPPPSSYYYCCCOOOOOOOSSSIICCCCCCCCCCCOPSSYYYCCCOOSSIISPPPP
PPPSSYYYYCCCOOOOOOOOSSIICCOOOOOOOOOPPSSYCCCOOOOOOSSIISSPPP
PPPSSEYYECCCOOOOOOOOSSIIIICCCCCCCCPPSSYCCCOOOOOOSSIISSPPP
PPPSSEYYECCCOOOOOOOOSIIICCOOOOOOOOOPSYCCCOOOOOOOSSIISSPPP
PPSSEYYYYEYYYYYYYCCCCCCCOOO        OOOSSSSSSSIIIIISSSIIISSPP
PPSSEYYYYEYYYYYYYCCCCCOOOO         OOOOSSSSSIIIIISSSIIISSPP
PPSSEYYYYEYYYYYYYCCCCCCCOOO        OOOSSSSSSSIIIIISSSIIISSPP
PPPSSEYYECCCOOOOOOOPSYCCHOOOOOOOOOOPSSYCCCOOOOOOOSSIISSPPP
PPPSSEYYECCCOOOOOOOPSSYCHOOOOOOOOOOOPPSSYCCCOOOOOOSSIISSPPP
PPPSSYYYYCCOOOOOOOOPSSYCCCCCCCCCCCCCPSSYCCCOOOOOOSSIISSPPP
PPPPSSYYYCCOOOOOOOPSSSYYCCCCCCCCCCCOPSSYYYCCCOOSSIISPPPP
PPPPSSYYYCCOOOOOOOPSSSYYCCCCCCCCCCOOOPSSYYYCCCOOSSIISPPPP
PPPPPSSYYYCCCOOOOPPSSYYYCCCCOOOOOOOOOPPSSYYYCCCOOOOPPPPPP
PPPPPSSYYYCCCOOOOPPSSYYYCCCCOOOOOOOOOPSSYYYYCCCOOOOPPPPPP
PPPPPSSSYYYCCCOOPPPPSSYYYCCCCOOOOOOOOOPPSSSYYYYCCCOOPPPPPPPP
PPPPPPPSSSSSSSSSSSYYYYYCCCCCCCYYYYYSSSSSSSSSSSSPPPPPPP
PPPPPPPPSSSSSSSSSSYYYYYYYYYYYYYYYSSSSSSSSSSSPPPPPPPPP
PPPPPPPPPPPPPPPSSSSSSSSSSSSSSSSSSSSSSSSPPPPPPPPPPPPPP
PPPPPPPPPPPPPPPPPPPPPPPPPPPPPPPPPPPPPPPPPPPPPPPPPP
```

Shade the Past

In the shade, stand, of my life,
I used to run but no more
I had teeth. Given weapons
To turn against their owners.
I used to.
In the shade, little room, like a cage
Walls of stone, window, light filters in,
And I avoid it, sit, don't strain
My eyes. I don't want to see.
I don't.
In the shade, standing, look, through leaves,
Cross the grounds, a visitor, for the owner.
No, not for me, no, go away, no, wait
Who is this, woman, dressed grandly,
Steps off the path, toward me.
Can I hide
From the shade, look, I recognize,
Saved her life, escape in the night.
Why is she here? How did she find me?
Why hello there young lady,
is the property owner in?"
Nod to her, and then, "Mother?"
I strain.

She smiles.
Finger to lips, leans in, whispers,
Returning a favour." Gives a sacchrine laugh.
Steps back. I reach out. "Wait."
She takes my hand. The past echos in.
And then, "We have a bit of business to get to."

"There Was a Soul"

There was a soul,
She came with outstretched arms.
She wracked herself, she wracked her mind.
She felt awake, she felt alive.

They say the soul is feminine, she is inside.
Take care of her; take care of your mind.

Echo through the forges of time,
The places where create,
Rather than find my time.
Wonder where you draw the line,
Walk along, see the sublime.
I faint, I can be unkind.
I wake, wonder, is it my time?

Tomorrow is coming, can I shift and become someone new?
Is it better that I shift and turn closer to you?
To become my own self,
To turn back to my soul.
She takes care of me,
I should take care of her too.

Wraith Hail

    The more of you that I inspected,
The more of you I wanted dead.
    But when I went to seek out myself,
I turned around, I was the slut.
    I'm in this, here, a room, I have a dictionary I have a bed.
You bought me too, paid food and drink,
    It takes a twist, the bed is red.
Tell me, what was I to you?
    I'm a scholar, and know the words,
I just...don't remember, let jog my mind; open the book:

    Definition of concubine in English:
    concubine
    NOUN
    Historical

1. (in polygamous societies) a woman who lives with a man but has lower status than his wife or wives.

        Example sentences
        'Abraham ended up with a wife and a concubine, Jacob with two wives and two concubines.'
        'Do they mean to train girls to becoming rich people's wives or concubines?'
        'Round about were the remains of two 20-year-old women (wives or concubines?), two 40-year-old men, and a dog.'
    1.1 archaic A mistress.
    Origin
    Middle English: from Old French, from Latin concubina, from con- 'with' + cubare 'to lie'.

It's funny, isn't it?

They used to tell me...know my place.

This isn't my place, is it?

It's only yours. It is Orion. his name, Orion.

There is a pile of papers and books in the corner,

Near my mother,

Who is insane, in the most loving sense,

"Gasoline was too expensive!" She sings, "I got kerosene~, ah, look! It doesn't smoke as much! How lovely!"

I watch the fire. I'll die here, impure. How many of my friends; they call it monogamy, but if you're not a wife, you're...concubine.

Let it burn me, mother Hail. The grandfather clock on the wall strikes twenty minutes of fire.

"Come now, don't be retarded, look, it's your man, calling in the hall!"

The flames are silent. They drift into the vents. The room is stone, it's stone, it's stone, it's...the tapestry, a gift from mom, catches fire, then the rug, just let me die.

"Come, Alexandre, darling, listen!"

The fire, I am a kēmist by training, kerosene, "it is a flammable liquid and the vapors can explode."

The air in the room ignites, a cold burst of red and yellow and orange and painful and mother help me

Enraged inside, I grasp my throat,

Enforce internal overload,

My cold hot rage,

My cold hard rage—

    HELP ME

Come dear, "she says," I am disoriented, my bed is singed, but it didn't catch. The rug is finding its way to me though. I'm dead.

"Come on, you can do it!"

I see her beckon. I hear from the hall, calls for his life. He doesn't call for me, the trash man. All the servants are out, he is alone, but for me.

"Let the wicked burn in hell, my love, we have work to do here yet! Can't you see them? They dance with the flames, the wicked, still, look! I want to join them, but my lovely, you still need taking care of, don't you?"

You can always trust a schizophrenic; if she's your mother.

I stand up, the bed catches, finally, sharing a moment of heat and lust with the rug. I don't see smoke, but I cough anyway.

"Look!" he enters the room, my mother is still not helping, she's helping, look, I look, I look, I loo-

"Hey, kiddo," I say to him, I say to Orion.

Orion, my owner, looks at me, he's frightened, paralyzed. He; I feel now, that my resentment was misplaced. He scans the books, on fire. I take the dictionary from the smoldering bed and add it to hell pyre (Zelos Wilder), and laugh as my mother does; the saccharin laugh of our family.

"Nice of you to join us, what's burning, did the vents do their job?" I stride to the window and open it. The flames feed on the oxygen, the atmosphere, my life.

"Everything! There was a burst in every ventilated room—"

I hated him, so I took him and threw him out the window,
Saved from the flames, I called out in flames.

Then my mother and I, we left the building and let it die,
die instead of me.

I'm more important.
I'm more important.

The Solune Prince - Chapter 6: The Assassin; or The Lussa Part 1

Before she left Alice and Finch's home, Chloe said, "When do you think I—"
"We!' said Alice.
"When should we put them up? Tonight?"
"Probably in the morning," Finch said.
"Before work!" Alice shouted.
"So, come by the same time you did today."
Chloe nodded, and exited, leaving the advertisements with them.

The clouds above, as well as what Chloe believed was a lack of moon beyond them made for an exceptionally dark night. Chloe had mapped out the city in her mind long ago, so she had nothing to worry about. *At least, I hope so.* As she walked, Chloe hummed the old Solune Royal Lullaby.

> *"—is what they say,*
> *Shed no tears is what they say,*
> *But my little baby, shedding tears you may*
> *Shedding tears you may.*
> *Your father's died the people say,*
> *Not coming back, so cry you may*
> *Your fathers died—"*

As she crossed between residential districts, rather unceremoniously, Chloe was grabbed from behind. Unable to see, she struggled and shouted.
"Guard!"
But she knew that there were none around. She had memorized the patrols as well as the streets; no one would be here for more than half an hour. Chloe steadied herself. She felt metal on her neck. *What do I do? And this to a prince! Why—*
"Are you the royal going to help the Lussa?"
What is this about?

Where did she come from?

Why me?

You ARE going to help the Lussa.

That makes her a stated enemy to, ah, to my current tasks, right?

Fight back.

Ah...

Chloe pushed her toes into the ground, steadying herself, and then pulled her hands in, grabbing the attacker's arm and digging her thumbs into the wrist. She heard metal hit the cobble and quickly took her assaulter's arms, pulled them forward and craned her own head straight and back. She heard the other person's face smack the back of her head; and pain ran through her own. *Ah, I hate that feeling.*

She turned around and, underwhelmingly, saw only a shadow of a person standing in the dark. It took a few steps back, rubbing its head.

It spoke, "If you leave the city, if you go north with Lilllith, we will kill you."

Chloe searched her waist. *Unarmed as usual...*

"Is that clear! Don't help the Lussa, we don't want it! We don't want you in the City."

It was clear to Chloe that this person was a woman, *and she seems to be young.*

Chloe stepped forward. Her foot hit something. *The dagger.*

"If Lillith makes here, then I will be returning with her." She said.

The shadow shifted, doing something with its arms.

With a single blunt word, it said, "No!" and dashed forward, cutting across with some sort of weapon. Chloe dropped to a kneel and pawed the ground for the knife. She kept her eyes up. She felt a slight wind pass above her head. She felt a sharp edge with her and took up the dagger with an overhand grip. She saw the woman's weapon glint as she recovered, a dull, thin sword.

"Damn it! Why is it so dark here?"

Chloe closed her eyes and opened her ears.

"Where are you! I... I can see you!" The assassin stammered, trying to seem in control, "I don't have to kill you, you know, just give you an injury severe enough that you don't take the trip. You know, send a message that—augh."

Chloe let go of the knife. It lodged firmly in what she assumed was the woman's thigh.

"Now, ah, now you have my message—you would do better to fight me in the bright of day."

The woman grunted through her teeth. Chloe took her by the shoulders, and kicked her legs out from under her. She fell, and Chloe followed her, dropping and pinning her to the stone path underneath her knee.

"So, who are you? What brings, ah, what brings you to my kingdom?"

Instead of answering, the woman, whose arms were still free, swung at Chloe. It was a slow and clumsy attack.

Make sure she does not cross us again.

—

Chloe let the blow hit her in the abdomen. The attacker, now detained, took this a sign of victory, and swung with her other hand, cutting across with the sword. Chloe pulled the dagger out of the woman's leg, blocked the attack with it, and then pushed it back into the wound.

"Ah," her voice writhed, "what did you—!"

"You have to keep it in to slow the bleeding."

She stood up and held the woman's chest underfoot, then stomped on the weapon with the other leg. To her surprise, the sword shattered into three pieces.

"What, ah, what kind of weapon is this?"

Chloe waited for a response, but got nothing. She said, "The guard will be here any second now. We will learn what we need from you—even if you do not speak. Your clothes, your skin, your blood, Natasha can read it all and learn what we want to know."

"No!"

The intonation was filled with terror, so much that Chloe began to question which of them was the assaulter. "What do you mean no? Why not?"

"I can't—you surviving is one problem, but then to be captured—no, they will abandon me! And then—"

"Then?"

Chloe knew the words weren't meant for her, but she figured she could pull something useful out of the hysteria. Instead, there was a long silence. Chloe couldn't tell the time that passed.

"L—just let me go."

Chloe looked down with condescension. For a moment, the clouds parted to reveal that there was in fact a moon in the night. They saw each other clearly in the silver light.

The attacker, assassin, the woman; she was very young, a girl almost. She couldn't have been any older than nineteen. Her hair was long and black as ash. Her skin, in contrast, was a slickly pale in colour, and her expression matched her tones, a face of desperation. There was something wrong with her eyes as well, but Chloe wasn't sure if it was just the dark of night. Her look sought Chloe's eyes for mercy. Never, in all her life, had Chloe been subject to such a request. Before she could make a silent reply, the clouds took over once more and they returned to the black.

"Tell me about yourself and, ah, I'll let you go after." Chloe addressed the darkness beneath her foot. "Why did you attack me?"

"Secret."

"What?"

"That's a secret!"

"Okay, what is your name then?"

"Secret!"

"Well then Secret, my is Chloe Rhye, Fifth Prince of the Solune."

"The Solune Prince!"

"Why are you here? To kill me?"

"Secret!"

Chloe put her other foot back down, and the girl finally spoke.

"There are those who oppose the Lussa crown."

"What is your name!"

"Secret!"

Chloe pressed her right foot down into the girl's chest. A threat.

"...Can you keep a secret?" She spoke in a tiny voice.

Chloe nodded, but then remembered how dark it was. "Yes."

"I am Ammalia. Don't tell anyone, especially not Ryann! I am Ammelia, a Lord of the Northern Quadrant."

"I will say I was attacked by a Lussa."

"Telling others that would... be in my best interest," said Ammelia.

Chloe frowned in the dark. She began to doubt whether she really should tell someone.

"...Now let me go?"

Chloe looked at the Lussa girl's face. Her vision was only now beginning to adjust. Whatever had been wrong with the girl's eyes before was currently gone.

"One more."

"—"

"How old are you?"

"Seventeen!"

She sounds like it. She even acts like it.

"Do not remove the knife until—" *How long do I have? Probably at least ten minutes before the guards come, I think.*

Five minutes later, Chloe finished dressing Ammelia's wound. She had removed the sleeves from her silk overcoat and created a makeshift badge from them. It seemed to her that she hadn't hit anything important or cut particularly deep, so it wasn't too difficult a procedure.

The last thing Ammelia said before leaving was, "Thanks" and "I'll see you the next time we attack you."

Chloe sighed, hoping that whoever Ammelia was referring to was as incompetent as she was. *Though I doubt it.*

The girl disappeared into the night, and shortly afterward, two guards showed up with torches. Chloe told them what happened, keeping the secret, but pointing to the shattered sword on the ground as evidence. A report was made, and then Chloe was offered an escort home, which she accepted.

The Capital

The country's iron face, I visit year after year

It is the nation's capital, reflecting the nation's fear.

Success and failure, here, concentrate, illuminated; heightened,

I'll show you what I mean soon, so don't you dare be frightened.

And so I give you all the bad news first,

Shrinking middle-class pockets, they always seem to thirst.

A city like this; the gap between privileged and vulgar at its worst.

The droning abstract masses manmade bureaucracies governments synthesize our curse.

Urban institutions manufacture, it would seem,

Politicians, always somehow sell us the obscene.

Mankind left and abandoned without interruption,

Leaving us thieves, drug houses, and corruption;

Yes, the successes of the cities are greater than its flaws,

Here it constructs new houses, in accordance with its laws.

They're investments for the wealthy, wealthy worry about the poor,

Who can take advantage high rent and own nothing, else live on someone's floor.

In the centre stands the courthouse and hall,

Conduits of virtue that stand reminding us all,

That bribery's a crime; only for those who can't afford it.

To fuel the machine's parts, is democracy and justice.

There was a pulse in every street, a human rhythm you could hear,

There was once a life in the steps my feet repeated year after year.

I don't think it will always be like it is today, and I am a bit afraid to say,

But maybe the robotic city could rediscover its heart one ecstatic blessèd day.

Pressing

He stands alone. Roaming for help. No allies east or west. A saddened nation.

Superstition washes over the West. Heresy. Host. Libel.

To persecute, you must dehumanize. A tactic remembered from the Trans-Atlantic Trade.

"The lack of instinct and narrow-mindedness of our upper classes,

Make the people an easy victim for this Jewish campaign of lies." (Adolf Hitler)

"Therefore be on your guard against the Jews, knowing that wherein

they have their synagogues, nothing is found but a den of devils in

which sheer self-glory, conceit, lies, blasphemy, and defaming of God and men

are practiced most maliciously and veheming his eyes on them." (Martin Luther)

Is the nature of the Jew hidden with secrecy, secrecy hiding malice?

It is the legacy of Rome, of laws, and of standards doubled, that keep minorities silent.

The Pope watches over the holocaust in silence, though the church founders said,

No more holocaust offerings will be made in the temple. They said no more sacrifices.

The First Rome destroyed the temple. Yoshke was not the final Jewish sacrifice.

Germany, the Third Rome, Third Reich, cleanses the weak and the faithfully deviant.

Can the Jew escape their pressing circumstances? Nuremberg is the law of Rome.

Would he find refuge west? But hadn't Spain, England, Poland, Lithuania, Portugal, Italy, France

Already made their decisions in the past? There will be no permanent Jewry here.

Where can a person of the book turn? Or should he turn his eyes downward,

And fall to the ground. Let him be taken by the neck, and strangled

By fumes. Poisons for the wretch, the creature, inhuman, inhumed.

But he will turn his eyes upward, and turn back to God, for, "The Lord has given,

and the Lord has taken away; Blessed be the name of the Lord." (Iyov 1:21)

And what of the haven, the New World?

Will they let in the Jew? Will they see the "light of the nations?" (Yeshayahu 49:6)

Would they save the landlocked "kingdom of priests?" (Shemot 19:6)

History records their answer: Why, yes of course; after he burns for the war.

The Long Haiku

Penny

I can imagine my children asking me, "What's a penny?"

Then one day we could travel to the United States and see a penny in real life.

Because Canada destroyed them years ago.

Worthy

Every time I read the words "You are worthy,"

A voice from heaven sounds inside my mind saying,

WORTHINESS IS NOT FOR YOU TO JUDGE.

The Book

They studied the item for decades. A sacred order formed to explore its secrets.

And then one day, an exile returned to the city, revealed a key, and unlocked it.

No one had considered it may be a lock. They hadn't even started developing a key.

Lussa Confederation [Excerpts]

With Translation

KING CERULLLUS, in the name of THE NAME, CREATOR of all lands: We the Priestly Poets address you; Progeny of the SOLLUSSA NATION; in council relating to the succession of thrones. Due to the horrific, and enstrifed histories of our people; especially of yours, who have known the land and its surroundings far longer; We, as councils of the CROWN; clerical and prophetic guides, and on behalf all estates of the LUSSA CITY STATE Including:

The Aristocrats of the East (who did defend against the ancient threat that split our nation twainwise), the Workers Guilds (who did so usurp the Workers Party for anti-political reasons), the Lawyers and Poets (who do craft the law, and do advocate as rhetoricians before the Judges), the Judges (who serve Justice), the Merchants and Traders, the Polits Officers, the Defense, the Voices of the Commons (who do so advocate for common People), and the Lords (who do so fight against the Voices of all People in Senate);

(These councils will hitherto be referred to as THOSE PREVIOUSLY MENTIONED.)

do hereby announce *w wiecznej pamięci sprawy* [in perpetual memorial of the matter]: AMENDATION In addition to all THOSE PREVIOUSLY MENTIONED, ROIIIIOUS (son of SAULLITE), successor to the throne; is acknowledged as a writer & signatory of the CONFEDERATION.

I. During this insecure time, living without an heir to our Throne; we, commanded by, and on behalf of, all THOSE PREVIOUSLY MENTIONED; have diligently sought at convention of Senate and Parliament, that we pursue the perseverance of the LUSSA STATE's peace, justice, order, commerce, defence, and spiritual connection. Therefore, by unanimous accord, and by the sacred vow unique to we the Priestly Poets, on behalf of THOSE PREVIOUSLY MENTIONED, hereby pledge, committing ourselves upon faith, decency, and conscience. . . .

II. Therefore the COMMONS, the POLITS, and the DEFENSE do vow to rise against every person or collection of persons who would choose and convene to cause tumult at an election. And since there is in our CITY STATE considerable dissidence between the two sects of the ROMANCE religion, (both PROPER, and GNOSTIC) to prevent any detrimental religious rebellion, as we have clearly seen in other realms [the Djeb], we do promise to ourselves that we who be *dysydenci religijni* [religious dissenters] (the GNOSTIC sect of the ROMANCE, as well as we the Priestly Poets and those who walk in and after our footsteps, followers of OLD) shall preserve the peace between ourselves and shed no blood out of differing faith and practices; nor shall there be any denial, or exclusion; be it under the pretext of a decree, or judicial ploy.

AMENDATION ROMANCE (PROPER) will be recognized as the State's official religion. The HERETICAL (here archaically labelled "GNOSTIC") sect will be subject to certain benevolent restrictions.

III. AMENDATION Law Three (III) is removed from the Confederation. Justification provided in future documents. . . .

V. We will instantiate a full democracy, to ameliorate the impending problem of the death of an heirless KING, and allow all those who are citizens to decide from among qualified citizens whom they wish to rule. In voting, we shall not prevent a person's action by coercion.

AMENDATION Law Five (V) applies only to the first vote. Law Five (V) implicitly suggests, using the words "among qualified citizens," someone who is related by blood to the MONARCH, even distantly. Let MONARCHS be encouraged to have many children to facilitate the justice of Law Five (V). . . .

END All of these things we promise to one another, and, upon signature, THE KING do promise to us, to be enduringly preserved and maintained under our faith, spirit, and honour. And against one who would wish to oppose this; to disturb the common peace and order, we shall, as a people, rise together and destroy. For greater assurance of all these things herein illustrated, we and all THOSE PREVIOUSLY MENTIONED, provide signatures and seals in our own hands.

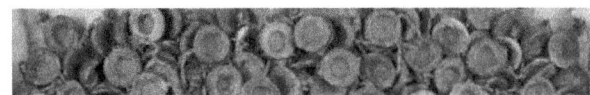

Dawngale and Zeth

Alice and Finch 2 (Preview / first chapter)

Alice was always a point of interest in the capital. During her childhood, she passively garnered followers, kids in the neighbourhood and later children from around the entire city. Alice was an energetic girl, and she grew into a tactful woman with an energetic flair. Though exiled for a few years during her youth, Alice returned to the city and became a member of the guard alongside Finch.

Finch was a scholarly boy, though he didn't know it. His father pressured him to read textbooks as a child because, well, his father homeschooled him, but also had to work. As a young adult, he worked in the guard in order to gain reputation so that he could find a way to get Alice back into the city. She hadn't done anything wrong, certainly not criminal enough to warrant an exile. She was simply discriminated against because she wasn't like them. She wasn't Solune like most of the people in the kingdom, but neither was she Riley. Alice Dawngale was of a different nation, she was a Plainkind. But Finch never really knew what that meant.

The difference was clear. Alice had an obvious and striking foreign look to her. Her bright yellow-pinkish hair was lighter and had less like the natural blonde common in Solune. Her eyes shone deep red, but when she got into a chase or a skirmish, the irises tightened into vertical slits, like a cat or reptile, and the colour brightened. Once, Finch got her energized and watched the change close up. He saw that it was blood coursing through capillary veins that caused the change. Nothing magical. In fact, everything that was out of the ordinary about Alice could be explained.

Finch had done a full study on her, to her dismay, a few months into their marriage. Alice had three sets of canines, longer and thicker than the Solune's. They often hid behind her oddly dark section of her cheeks. This part of her face pulled back, allowing for her to open her jaw unusually wide. Her front teeth consisted of two fangs pointing downward, followed by four more, two on each side, pointed up. In the middle, regular incisors, but with angled fronts. When she smiled, her cheeks also pulled back, and this could be quite terrifying for people who didn't know her. Her nails were not only long, but animal like and dark. They were unmistakably weapons for hunting.

And so, while Alice was exiled, he tried his best to find out about the Plainkind. That was where Chloe Rhye came in. She was part of the royal family, but had offered to teach him and some of his peers. She gave him firsthand accounts from before the kingdom was secluded behind giant walls by the King.

"The Plainkind...they are a ferocious people. I've met a few, but we had little in common. A few centuries ago when my mother was colonizing the surrounding area, the Elken Jungle, N'Tariel Plains, and the Plainkind Desert were the only places she could not conquer. We've relinquished our control since then, but even so. Their weapons are for hunting, but they are both heavier and sharper than ours. It seems they mine. But primarily they hunt, and what they hunt are large beasts—dinosaurs."

Finch was walking home from his lab. He thought back to his childhood. Where had all of his peers gone? What had they done with their lives? He had returned to his education after Alice was allowed back into the city, but the only person he met in the University was Artus. Jutt had gone missing, and...who else was there, really? It was Artus who first introduced him to the "monster" of Murdock City, to Alice.

Finch was walking home with an armful of books. Unlike when he was a child he no longer read Natural Studies textbooks, or even books from outside of the kingdom, by academics such Joss Resz the N'Tariel, Bradley Jeremy the East Metch, or Azure Shion of the West. Now, he kept up with the scientific literature of his field, kemia, also called chemistry.

"Aww...I think I took too much again." Finch stopped on the cobbled street, near a house.

The door in front of him opened, and a youthful woman with giant teeth smiled serenely and took the books.

"Oh Finch, I think you've lost strength since your guard days. I remember you used to be stronger than me!" Alice said. She put the books down on a piece of furniture that had been crafted especially for material from his work. At least, like his father, Finch could do work around the house.

He frowned, closing the door behind him. "Alice, I think you're right. You know Riley tend not to be very strong anyway. We, shameful but true, we tend to sneak around in the night."

"I know." Alice was cooking, which was always an ordeal. She used the stove in such a dangerous way. It was a normal cooking stove, with a fire inside and removable elements to bridge and make consistent the heat. But Alice always removed the elements and played with the fire as she cooked. Today was no different.

Finch stared at her suit of armour. "How was work today?"

"Oh, well, interesting you ask. We encountered your cousin, Dirge."

"Dirge?" Finch thought for a moment. Dirge was his middle name, his mother's name. "Wait, Jutt?"

"Yes, remember her? She was a little older than us. I thought she was a boy when we met because her hair was so short. Well it turns out she turned to crime." Finch was shocked. The spices Alice was frying caught fire. "Ah!" She put the lid on, waited, and then opened it up and added in chunks of meat.

"Oh. I...I actually knew that. Her and her mother."

"Yes, well, she's working with Natasha Rhye now. The Prince. She's my boss, by the way, that's how I know."

"Huh."

"They want me." Alice moved the pan onto a proper element and added vegetables in.

"What do you mean?" Finch came nearer to her.

"Natasha says I should join the agents. They need more people in the west."

"The west? Isn't that—"

"—where they had the revolution. The whole thing with the shares. It's gotten really authoritarian and the Solune figure that the couple agents we have there aren't enough. They want someone strong. They want a Plainkind agent in there."

"Really?"

"I'm perfect, Natasha said. The Djeb is full of Plainkind like the Solune kingdom is full of Riley. A visible minority. That means that for the most part, I would fit in. But Finch..." She put the element back on the stove and closed the drafters, and then covered the food. "I don't want to leave this city again. You worked so hard to get me in. I like being a guard, not a King's Agent."

"It is a great honour to work for the King directly. And...weren't we always talking about this?"

Alice turned to him, her eyes a sharp red. "What do you mean?"

"Going west. That's...that's where the Plainkind are."

"My father!" Alice covered her mouth, and then her eyes. She sat down at the dining table.

Finch looked at the food. It was nearly done. He moved it off the stove and joined her at the table.

"...It is finally time, isn't it Finch. Finally time to return to my home. I haven't been there since I was four or five. Since my mother..."

"Since your mother saved your life. I know. And I think it is time. The walls have finally opened. Chloe Rhye said that the Lussa have become new allies, and they are closely connected to the Djeb through trade. Revolution aside, it is likely safer there than it has been thanks to that new alliance."

"Finch you have to come."

"Of course!" Finch stood up. "I—"

"No, become an agent with me."

"I—" Finch stopped. He breathed for a few minutes, and then stood up and prepared the food.

He returned to the table with two plates and utensils. Alice ignored the food, she stared only at him. Finch sat down and took three, then four, deep breaths.

"According to my studies, it takes around four months to get back into shape."

Alice grabbed her husband's arm. "Finch they will train you!"

String Quartet

From The Journal of Anselm Siren, Eight day, 08/008. Approved for release by both Sirens.

Marriage, the final frontier; the highest way of knowing. The perfect spouse, the soul mate, according to Divine Law, is the one whom you marry. There is no other criterion.

My wife would rise in the middle of the night on some nights, the long nights, and wander to the doorway. Sometimes, she would linger long enough for me to stir. Other times, she exited with the silent speed cultivated in her past life. I would feel her movement during the lighter portions of my sleep. There is a period after midnight when the body enters a lighter phase. As the nights grow longer in the dark season, so does this phase. I have heard from the priestly poets that some awaken during this time to pray or meditate. Based on her abrupt increase in skill, I gauge that she had been waking since last winter.

Once, I woke up and saw her creep out of the room. I sat up and followed. We ambled past the two rooms belonging to the children, and then through the kitchen. Where was she going, I wondered. We moved past the front door, along a white papered hallway, to the other end of the house. When I saw that she held the key, I finally understood. We weren't going outside, we were going into the addition, the room kept locked away from the children.

She grabbed the door handle and then tried to pull away suddenly. Her skin stuck to the iced metal. She sucked in a breath. "You do it, Anz." I should have known she had noticed me. Even as we reached our thirties, Alexandre's instincts remained sharp. I took the key and opened the door. The annex was nearly as cold as outside. "Anz, it's cold." I wasn't sure if she was trying to be cute, but then she added, "fix it."

I frowned, but closed the door behind us and moved to the small stove in the corner. The moon filtered in through the high windows and choice skylights. This was, despite its purpose, built to be private. Even though it was around the size of a bedroom, most of the space was filled with wires, which tonight glinted in the celestial light. An iced glow covered the area from wall to wall, illuminating the frosted metal strings that cut across the room at various angles and heights. I filled the stove with wood shavings and lit it. "How long—"

"These strings are too cold to play. I am going to be out of tune."

I stocked the wood stove and barred the door. "Not for long."

"I know." She swam through the wires skilfully, like a spideress in her web. Once in place, she struck a string. It hit a sharp note. "Oh yes, this is...just awful."

This room was added for the sole purpose of housing her instrument. I had thought that Alexandre, like other middle-class women, would want a room to read novels and play cards in; to have tea with other women. Perhaps she'd park a harpsichord in the corner to entertain guests. I should have known her better. This was no guest room, it could barely fit our family.

A note rang out.

"Oh listen!" She giggled. "I knew it! The tuning, la! I have been uptuned, it sounds like a full step down." She struck an E-minor chord.

"Full step up, not down," I said. "Actually, step and a half. You're playing sharp."

"Oh. I think you're right Anselm." She strummed a power chord and smiled and sang a note through black metal teeth. Her silver eyes shone in mine with the lust of moon. "They're sticking to my fingers like the door."

We invested in this project a couple of years ago. The result was this room-sized instrument, laid out like a series of harps. It wound dangerously from wall to wall. Some came across at a level plane, and others were strung diagonally across the pilot's left or right. When Alexandre stepped in, the piano wire lay before her in large sets of twenty-four and thirty-six, and small sets of eight, exactly like a harp. We needed at least a full octave per set, so one could start play at any location and find the notes they needed. Most of the metal hung comfortably around Alexandre's waist, while sharps and flats hovered by her head and down by her thighs.

"Wait, if these are in sharp, I could probably play something...heavy."

"Aren't you afraid you might wake them up?"

"No..." She slid her playing gloves on and began to strum aggressively. Four D-sharps, followed by E-sharp and A-sharp simultaneously. "We're on an exterior wall, remember?"

As she played, repeating E sharp notes until she hit A flat, the heat of the room began to affect the strings. Her notes got lower in pitch until the instrument was creaked back into tune. She used to play bare-fingered, but she decided—and I didn't argue—that she would shield them. Let them get soft for once in her life. I took her bid and stitched gloves from a thin, tough material. She is right to use them, now that we have a homestead and some peace.

It was only half a decade ago that she and I travelled from empire to kingdom selling our accolades and swords to the nearest ruler. Mercenary work and the royal hire weren't the first time she'd had to do battle either. Her fighting skill came from a time in her life that was darker, when she was the maiden Alexandre Dirge. I could see that past in her as she played. It seemed to me that, to some extent, she tends to let herself fall into violent situations. However, once she had the favour of the new Monarch, Her Serenity King Janna Rhye, I think Alexandre finally had the excuse she needed to turn down her old line of work and do something else with her talents.

Alexandre started playing a tune that was new to me, sombre notes she must have practiced on previous nights. She hammered higher notes with her right hand, holding a melody with the piano wire. Lower notes she strummed on bass strings with her left hand. She swept across sets of strings arranged specifically for playing these sorts of chords one-handed. The chords kept rhythm, sounding like an aged guitar underneath the melody. Occasionally, Alex would find time between longer sustained chords to visit other strings with her left hand, harmonizing the melody. I listened, experiencing her emotions sympathetically.

"What inspired this?" I called quietly.

"It was…"

I could feel the sorrowed chords and the melancholy that sang out in the song. It was a work unfinished, and I could tell she'd only practiced it a few times. And as I listened, I began to also watch; paying close attention, especially to the rhythm and incomplete harmonies. As she played on, I stood. I strode around the instrument and slid in beside her. She, taking my cue, began repeating a portion of her song so that I could find my footing and test the strings. I started moving my hands along with hers, and apart from hers. I found an accompanying rhythm with my left hand. My right briefly tangled with her fingers as I took over the harmony, building on what she had struggled to do with only two hands. Once we had found our places between each other inside the instrument, she stopped repeating the song and we continued it instead. Alexandre's right hand danced delicately across the wires and I improvised along. The strings soothed a grief I didn't know I had, perhaps one that wasn't mine at all. Alexandre was smiling and shedding silent tears. The two of us completed the instrument; two people, playing four parts. This was it, this is the String Quartet.

"…'Addicted to Chaos.' Remember that you said…" She began to hum.

Alexandre shifted and her left hand played a new pulsing rhythm as we moved into the last section of the song. We reached the climax, and I adapted as smoothly as I could. It was a little faster now, and the music was less intricate and more intense. I felt the heat of the room and the heat of our motions. When I looked over to Alexandre, I saw that her tears had been washed away by perspiration. She pushed into the pulse of the song, over and over until she struck a set of notes three times in succession, and moved her hands to block me from playing further.

"This is where it stops," she breathed.

I looked around, surrounded by the Quartet. The stove was running low. "This room will get cold again. It might be good to return before dawn."

"Yes," she murmured. We climbed out and she wiped her face, flushed deep through pale features. She took a step into me and grabbed my back. "My heat. I am overcome."

"Where it stops?" I took the hand that had stopped our playing. "This is where it starts."

"My my! Away with us! Take me from this place, Anselm." Alexandre laughed, and her black teeth shone in the moonlight. She ran to the door.

"As you wish." Leaving the smoldering stove, Alex, smitten, locked the door behind us.

The Solune Prince – Chapter 41-42: Regimen I-II

"What's it called when you cry on someone's shoulder, then they never speak to you again?"

She sat on the lush rug, looking sad with her freshly acquired bruise.

"What are you going to tell them, when you return with a black eye?"

"There is no them."

Alexandre looked over at the Lussa girl. "There was."

"There was, yes. Now, I am 'them.' I will retake my father's house, and I will relive his legacy. Something from nothing."

"You are a horrible killer, but you're hardly nothing Ammelia."

"Thanks—ah! Let go!"

"What is this?"

"It's—" the pale girl paused, flushing down to her toes. "That's one of my horns."

"What are you?"

"We...I don't know Alex, but my father was the same. My brother too. He never..." She started to cry, and then whispered, "...he never cut his off in cowardice like I did."

"They're poking through your hair a little."

"I know. I haven't touched them since we first met...I was going to after returning but..."

"You are no longer a coward."

Ammelia continued crying.

—

"Shalla, you're cooking for one more today."

"I am? Who?" Shalla looked around, but only saw Alexandre's backside as she left.

—

"I could, but I am really not sure what she knows already."

Alexandre shrugged. "Almost nothing."

Lilllith nodded. "I guess Siren could use a sparring partner. Senica may not have a lot of kill pressure, but she has years of defensive training. Siren could use someone more his level."

"Really? You can tell that about the Djeb girl just through that one fight?"

"Yes. She is not at all accustomed to proper fighting, but she is very very well practiced. I would say she started a couple years after puberty."

"Hmm."

—

Kent was napping on a bench out back in the giant forest they called an estate. Senica was trading punches with Astore. Slow, and deliberate, but with no force behind them.

"Senica, I think you're better at this than me. You should have gotten a better rating when you fought Lilllith."

Senica blushed and stumbled, hitting Astore in the face as she fell. She caught herself, and Astore rubbed his cheek. "Oh umm. My apologies. I don't really use weapons. I know a little spear or polearm, but that's it."

"So you know how to hit people with a stick?" Alexandre called out from the back door. She approached them, leaving the back door of the building open behind her.

"Yes." Senica nodded, and then looked up thoughtfully. "You could say that I guess."

Astore glared at the door. Ammelia poked her head out, and they locked eyes. "Yip!" She hid again.

"Is that the killer in there? Alexandre I think you're being hunted."

Alexandre shrugged and sat down next to Kent. She glanced back at the door, and then to Astore, who was still staring.

"She's with me now."

"Sounds like a trick to me."

—

Chloe Rhye was woken up by Annissette. It took around six tries, which was similar to her success with Anselm Siren.

"Are all you Solune so lazy? Hmph!" The small girl crossed her arms. She was wearing an old fashioned large, grey, flowy dress. Old fashioned in the sense that it went to her ankles and wrists, covering most of her neck.

Chloe mumbled something again, and then sat up. "I got back late...let me—"

"Nope! Lilllith said you need to get on her routine. You will be learning to fence every day from now on."

"Every day!"

"Well, you'll get one or two days off to heal."

"Heal!"

Chloe looked like she was about to cry. Like she was a child again. In fact, she had given Annissette childish vibes all morning.

"Come, grow up. It's the same thing the rest of us went through."

Chloe jumped up. She was wearing a blue nightdress with short sleeves and nothing else. "Really? So you can fight then?"

"Of course. A maiden must keep herself safe."

Chloe grabbed her. It was supposed to be a hug, but the Solune, being over six feet tall and unusually broad, couldn't properly hug her spontaneously, so it ended up as a grab. Annissette blushed. She could feel Chloe's soft skin, and strong arms. It was a weird mixture, like an old farm mother who got strong lifting sheep out of the ditches and hauling straw and doing laundry.

When Chloe was done, she leaned back and looked down at the girl. "You're over a head shorter than me."

Annissette sputtered, and then just left.

"Lilllith is expecting you for breakfast soon. Get dressed!" She called back through the room.

—

"Who's that?"

"It's Ammelia. She's my new friend."

Siren stared at the girl, who was wrestling with Senica, and then looked back at Alexandre.

"You're glowing."

"I..." Alexandre slowly raised her eyes to meet his. "I'm what?"

"Hmm?"

"Hmm?"

"I said you look beautiful this morning." He looked back at the two young women fighting. Kent was actively engaged for once, but it seemed he was watching his wife intensely...almost creepily. Siren just stared amused.

"I what?"

Alexandre, who had almost never been complimented in her life, had no idea what was happening or how to respond.

"I think you look very good in light coloured sun dresses. It accents your raven hair."

"Raven..." Alexandre blushed and pulled her head into her neck.

"I'll take it. I was going to go until you said something intelligible."

"I...what?" Alexandre felt a rush through her psyche. "Siren don't say things like that."

"Fine, I'll say something mean."

Alexandre waited.

"You usually look ragged. Half dead with sleep deprivation and stress. But today, you look radiant, and you have this cute little dress on instead of...well to be honest, I don't mind the clothes that show off your figure either."

Alexandre waited more.

"I know we've already met, but I was impressed with how you've handled the journey so far. It seems like you've done more than all of us apart from Chloe combined. You're impressive. I like you. Is this morning somehow different?"

"I slept in a bed for one." Alexandre placed her fingers on her forehead, covering her eyes. "And I give Ammelia that eye."

"Oh, yeah...she's looking a little roughed up. I thought it was the wrestling."

"No, I thought she was doing another attack but...she didn't even have a weapon on her."

"Interesting."

"Hey hey!" A sweet yet commanding feminine voice cut through the meadow. "Stop a second."

Senica dismounted Ammelia, who was losing by a large margin. *Lilllith was right.* Chloe approached the visitor and took hold of one of her horns in her fingertips.

"What is this?" Chloe said.

Ammelia sighed resentfully. "You're the second person to do that exact thing, and ask that exact question."

Chloe tilted her head and half smiled. "What did you tell the first person? And who is this individual imitating me?"

"Horns. They're little horns. I usually cut them off."

"One of your parents is from the far south?"

Ammelia's world froze.

Chloe Rhye, Fifth Prince of the Solune, stood in front of her, taking in the sun and smiling. Her skin was lightly tanned, not pale. Her eyes were a deep brown. A brown, Ammelia felt, somehow deeper than the sky. She looked like a kindhearted aunt, the sort who would babysit you when your parents wanted to go on a date, and then bake you cookies and play games. *Where did she come from? Where did I come from?*

"Where did you say?"

"If you...cross the sea from the Djeb and head south many days. There are ancient records of a race of goat-horned people with wide eyes just like a herd animal. That is you, is not it? But your eyes are normal."

"My father is half Lussa so I am..."

"I see. I have long wondered what it is like to look through such eyes but...I cannot speak to sheep."

"N-neither can I."

Chloe laughed. "Of course not. What happened to your eye? Are you not here to attack me again? You are doing a poor job."

"Alexandre. No."

Chloe looked back at Alexandre, but didn't say anything. The other woman seemed to be smitten with her partner. *How unexpected.*

"Food!" A deep voice boomed across the field and echoed back off the trees. It was Rockk.

"Well, let us go Ammelia."

—

"I would like to point out, youth."

"Ammelia."

"Ammelia, that though it was unnecessary because Shalla always cooks too much, Alexandre asked her to make enough for you anyway."

"I don't know how much she makes, this is my first time here."

"And what happened to your eye, child?" Lilllith continued.

"Imprudence."

Lilllith raised an eyebrow. "Good answer. Have you been educated, youth? I know that women's education is often neglected."

"I had a wide liberal education."

"Fair." Lilllith took a forkful of the same side from the other day, that rice. "Rockk, you are on for supper. Don't be late today."

"I'll see," the young man shrugged.

Lilllith shook her head. "And will you be moving out soon?"

Rockk frowned. "I don't think so, not soon. Not as much work as one might hope in the courts recently."

"Almost as if it's being swept under the rugs..." Col mused.

"That, or that the nobles, who usually duel to first blood for honour and take each other to court for minor infringements, have been doing so less. They are up to something."

"Yes they are," Alexandre said through a mouthful of food. Lilllith, who was seated near her, slapped her wrist. "Phwhat."

"Ammelia, what were you taught?"

"History, biology, arithmetic, algebra—"

"You have algebra here?" Alexandre said, rubber her wrist, her mouth clear.

"Yes..."

"But the East Metch invented that. Do you have contact with them?"

"Who?"

Kent was nodding even before Senica started to speak. "The East Metch and the Djeb have some contact through the Sol-Metch State. That's where me and Kent were staying. It's mostly traders, but a lot of scholars like to travel to learn in the East Metch and vice versa."

"Vice versa," Kent nodded the foreign words that almost no one in the room understood.

Ammelia shrugged, "singing, a bit of harpsichord, rhetoric, angleometry, logic, theology, astronomy and literature."

"Your education system is diffuse then? It isn't formalized into seven?" asked Chloe, who had long finished not only her first plate but a second and third.

"No."

"You didn't study laws?" Rockk asked.

"I did, but only enough to stand up for my honour in court. You know, noble things."

Rockk shook his head. "That explains why you need us. You nobles are horrible at defending yourselves."

"I suppose I will have to learn Lussa law, at least a bit." Chloe murmured, thinking deeply.

"It would be a good idea," Rockk said. "How much do you know of your own system?"

"Well, I can serve as a poet, which is similar to your lawyer, in a Solune court. I have, a few times."

"Really!"

"Beyond Solune, I know common law, and the Old Book."

Rockk and Lilllith stared at Chloe. Annissette and Alexandre saw them, and so they did the same.

Lilllith let Rockk talk. "You know the Old Book? How?"

Chloe once again cocked her head. "What do you mean how? I brought a copy with me."

"What!" Rockk stood up and left the room. "No way!" they heard him call out down the hall. Lilllith stood and followed him.

Seeing that everyone was done, Shalla and Col, stood, bowed, and started to collect the plates.

"What did I do?"

Annissette said, "Chloe, the Old Book, assuming we're talking about the same one, is an ancient and partially destroyed artifact here."

"Destroyed?"

"By age. We have preserved maybe half of it."

"Oh. Well I have the whole thing."

"You do understand how this might rend someone's psyche, right? We've built layers on top of what we have, but the complete edition could ruin centuries of law and custom." Annissette shrugged.

"You speak as if this isn't really your problem," Senica said.

"Well...it sort of isn't. We in the lower classes live close to reality. It's the theory junkies, the nobles, lawyers, and scholars, who will have issues. In fact, I bet they will oppose or even destroy your copy."

"I can always ask for another."

Astore smiled. "I am a stealth courier after all. I can move across land twice the speed of a conventional runner."

Chloe nodded once, with intent.

Back

Daniel Triumph 2020
Director of Chochma Arts Ltd.
Owner of www.danieltriumph.com

Daniel Triumph

You can contact me in these places,
Feel free to reach out!

@danielltriumph (instagram, facebook, twitter)
www.danieltriumph.com

CPSIA information can be obtained
at www.ICGtesting.com
Printed in the USA
BVHW021425280623
666442BV00013B/457